FATED TO THE DRAKARN COMMANDER

DRAKARN MATES
BOOK 4

KATE RUDOLPH

Drakarn warrior, deadly enforcer, feared mentor, and shield to the weak in a world of molten rock and razor-sharp wings, this is what I am. I never waver... until she crashes into my fortress and demolishes every ironclad rule I've ever held.

Hawk is human: smaller than my kind, yet braver than any warrior I've ever known. From the instant her scent sears my senses, I know two truths: she is mine, and I will break worlds to protect her.

But forging a bond with an alien female inflames ancient grudges and council politics—each side eager to shred our alliance before it blooms. And when enemy forces appear demanding human blood, there are those in Scalvaris eager to give her up.

They call me ruthless for locking her in my

private quarters, for guarding her every step, but she's too precious to lose.

Rival clans plot war, temple priests preach doom, and eagle-eyed enemies circle for the kill. I'll face them all—wings flared, claws bared—to keep her safe.

A Drakarn's mate isn't a choice. She's fate. And a Drakarn warrior never surrenders what belongs to him.

KHORLAR

The echo of grunts and impacts reverberated through the training caverns, each sound a percussive slap against the rough-hewn walls. The air hung heavy, thick with the tang of sweat, superheated rock, and the acrid burn of overworked leather from strained armor.

I stood perched on a rocky outcropping, arms crossed. Below, trainees sparred with varying degrees of competence, most displaying defensive formations as porous as the atmosphere above Volcaryth. A flicker of impatience ignited in my chest—an almost instinctive urge to snarl corrections or bark orders. I suppressed it. Not yet. Let them taste failure, scrape their hides raw. They'd learn more from bruises than lectures.

My gaze moved restlessly between sparring pairs, weighing their intent against clumsy execution. Bad habits, unchecked now, would bleed them dry later. A head thrown too far back during a strike, a tail dragging where it should provide balance ... my patience frayed, but remained, for the moment, intact.

Then my gaze drifted, pulled across the cavern to the far side: the humans.

They weren't sparring Drakarn today. Their exercise centered on scaling the treacherous rock faces, navigating the uneven terrain with a painstaking focus. Boots scraped against sharp edges and loose rubble, their small, strange hands finding purchase along jagged holds. Where my kind relied on tails for balance and powerful wings for controlled descents, the humans compensated with an unnerving precision, gripping tighter, crouching lower. It wasn't natural—it couldn't be, for them—but they were relentless.

One caught my attention.

Red hair pulled back under a utilitarian leather band, a face that radiated composure despite the exertion evident in every controlled movement. It wasn't unusual for me to observe the humans as they moved through the caverns; curiosity was simply practicality draped in the guise of observation.

But this one ... she was singularly focused. Intent.

She studied the rock face before her as though it were a puzzle to be solved, not merely an obstacle to overcome. A sharpness edged her gaze, darting and aware, registering movement and depth in ways I hadn't noticed in the others.

Without conscious intent, I edged closer to the platform's edge, my breath measured as I watched her ascend. She was precision incarnate ... until she wasn't. One of those leather boots dislodged something loose, a hairline crack spider-webbing across the rock face in an instant.

Then everything happened almost too fast for reaction.

The crack widened, a series of sharp pops and snaps that broadcast disaster as physics caught up. Her hand shot upward, grasping for a higher hold. She didn't scream, didn't freeze, but some instinct drove her to try and stabilize as the rock beneath her gave way.

First, loose stones slammed against the cliff face, falling in an uncontrolled cascade. Then, her body followed, moving too fast. She twisted mid-air, clawing desperately for purchase, but collided hard against another outcropping several feet below. Another slip, a mere inch more, and she'd have plunged off the ledge into oblivion.

The rockfall wasn't stopping. Dust clouded the dim light, obscuring her small, curled form.

"Damn it." The words were a low growl, ripped from my throat.

Instinct surged, burning white-hot, obliterating every other thought. My claws scraped against the rock as I launched myself forward. Survival demanded timing, precise calculation—not reckless action—and yet there I was, abandoning calculation entirely.

My kind did not make mistakes on terrain like this. My hands gripped the heated rock, tighter than iron, carving a path downward with an unforgiving mix of force and control. The stones that had crumbled toward her still rained around us.

Her scent hit then. Even amidst the acrid chaos of dust and falling debris, it struck me like a whip. I refused to acknowledge the sensory jolt, the sudden hypersensitivity that flared on my tongue.

Everything sharpened, refocused, like a lightning bolt had struck me.

Her scent was closer now: crisp and alien, deceptively light, yet sharp enough to draw blood. Beneath the atmospheric noise of the cavern, I could almost hear the frantic beat of her pulse—faint but rapid, defying her outward composure.

The last few feet were the most treacherous. Sharp, jagged stones forced an awkward perch, wings momentarily extending for balance as dirt and gravel shifted. Any lesser warrior would pause, regroup, resist the urge to charge blindly.

No time for that.

Seconds mattered. Less than that.

Then she was there—fingers white-knuckling a warped, unstable ledge that offered no real security. A smear of blood at her knuckles. A precarious over-hang threatened to collapse near her left leg. I landed close, but not close enough, not yet at her side.

This place offered no kindness, no quarter.

"Don't move!" My voice thundered, an imperative, not a request.

Everything else dissolved as I extended my clawed hand to her. Any sweetness lingering beneath her scent was ruthlessly ignored, my focus narrowing to raw efficiency as I sought a more secure foothold. The chaos subsided, leaving lingering instability in its wake.

I pulled her away from the ledge.

The world narrowed to the visceral—the grit of her bloodied hands slipping against my claws, the searing heat of the broken rock, her weight against my grip. Every sense screamed for focus, demanding I lock down instinct and channel it into precision.

The tension in my chest ratcheted tighter, some unseen thread pulling at a place I hadn't had time to name—something wild and ancient, testing the limits of my control as her scent flooded the space between us, closer this time. My tongue burned as if branded, the acrid metallic tang of danger mingling with her phantom sweetness.

This was not the moment for distraction—damned if my own body didn't agree—but the sensation was suffocating, scalding. It deepened as I wrapped my other clawed hand around her waist, sharp focus overriding any resistance. No matter how fast I worked, the heat radiating off her lingered, clinging to me.

"You weigh less than an ash cat," I grunted, hauling her upward. "Stop fighting me."

"I'm not fighting!" she hissed, her voice sharper than expected. She kicked her legs toward the collapsing rubble below, struggling for a foothold. I swore and pulled harder, drawing her body flush against mine.

"Then stop squirming!" I snapped.

The moment her weight fully shifted into my grasp, the tension snapped—not just in the rock, but somewhere deeper in me. My tail flicked against the edge of the ledge as I propelled us upward, clearing the worst of the debris. My wings flared briefly, catching the air to stabilize us, and finally—finally—we landed on solid footing.

Her breath hitched, the first unguarded sound of emotion slipping past her carefully constructed exterior. For a moment, we were utterly still. Dust settled in the faint light, coating her bruised and dirt-streaked skin like motes of gold.

Her scent lingered. Unforgivingly.

"Are you injured?" My voice was gruff, harsher than intended.

Her chest rose and fell rapidly. She tilted her head slightly, those sharp, assessing eyes locking onto mine like she was calculating some equation that couldn't be spoken aloud.

"Nothing broken," she rasped, exhaustion evident in her tone. "Thanks."

There it was—a flicker, a crack barely noticeable, as if she'd loosened her grip on the vigilance she wore like armor. When her fingers brushed briefly against the clawed hand still gripping her waist, I felt her relax.

That wouldn't do. Not here. Not now.

Not with *her*.

"Be more careful next time," I ground out, my voice cracking like a whip. Without ceremony, I released her, the distance I needed achieved as she staggered slightly to her feet. She didn't fall, though; her legs steadied quickly, and she held herself like a queen.

Her expression shifted imperceptibly, mouth settling into its former sharp line. The momentary vulnerability I'd glimpsed dissolved as quickly as it had appeared.

Good. Better this way.

She took a breath, her jaw working as if considering something to say before closing her mouth again. Straightening her spine, she moved stiffly past, her scent trailing after her like smoke.

I stood rooted, my chest tightening under the weight of it all—her scent, the phantom warmth of her body pressed against mine, the impossible ache that clawed through me like something ancient trying to awaken.

It couldn't awaken. It wouldn't.

The burn on my tongue refused to fade.

By the time I'd reached the platform, the human was gone, slipping back into the tighter-knit cluster of her kind near the edge of the training ground. Where she belonged.

One of the Drakarn trainees glanced toward me, worry etched on his uncalloused face. A warrior fresh to the field, still too tender to hide his questions beneath a stoic mask. I bared my teeth briefly in warning, and his gaze darted away. They would learn, in time, to stop looking for cracks in their instructors—or at least to hide when they did.

I forced myself to focus on the Drakarn trainees. I was not responsible for the humans, and that wouldn't change.

But the burn in my chest refused to fade, no matter how much I tried to ignore it.

1

KHORLAR

THIS WAS MADNESS.

The heat was an assault, waves shimmering off the scorched earth around our pathetic excuse for a camp. It promised brutality for the trainees. Good. Let the fire bake endurance into their soft hides.

Behind me, the guttural rumble of Drakarn voices grated against the too-smooth cadence of the humans. It was grit under my scales. This whole exercise reeked of folly. Dragging untested warriors outside of Scalvaris was risky enough.

Adding *them*? Madness.

I turned, scanning the camp. Trainees moved with the hesitant precision of students afraid of screwing up. Their fear was a familiar scent, almost comforting in its predictability. They'd learn the unforgiving honesty of this world, or they'd feed it.

The humans ... they moved with an alien fluidity that still set my teeth on edge after all these months. Terra gestured sharply at Lexa over some scrap laid out like a battle plan. Vega stood sentinel, her eyes missing nothing, a grudging spark of respect kindled despite myself. My warriors were untrained. These women? They were battle tested and bloodied.

But they still didn't belong here.

Then my gaze snagged on *her*.

Hawk.

Kneeling by her pack, her movements were spare, precise. Lethal economy. The light struck sparks off her dark skin, her shorn hair seemed to drink in the light and swallow it whole. She swiped sweat from her brow, a simple gesture that sent a jolt through me.

My tongue scraped raw against the roof of my mouth. My fangs *ached* with a sudden, burning throb.

Hells.

I ripped my gaze away, jaw clamped hard enough to crack stone.

"Stone Fist, sir." Marvok approached, wings held tight. The kid's scales had barely hardened. "The perimeter checks are complete."

"And?" The word was a growl ripped from my chest, the distraction welcome.

He flinched. "Tracks. North. Small predators—"

"Nothing is *small* out here." I snarled the words, pinning him with my stare until he looked away. "Double the watch."

He scrambled back. Untested. Maybe not hopeless. He'd learn or he'd die.

Volcaryth was a harsh place. There was no room for softness when it came to training, not if I wanted to keep my warriors alive.

My eyes betrayed me again, snapping back to where Hawk was.

Had been.

Now the space was empty. Vega was gone too.

Wrongness coiled in my gut, cold and sharp.

Stealth was instinct. I moved through the camp, silent as death, hunting her scent. When it hit me— that sharp, foreign sweetness cutting through the dust and heat—the reaction was a physical blow. My fangs pulsed again, a searing agony radiating deep into bone.

My tongue burned as if I'd tasted magma. Only this heat I craved more and more.

It was a brand seared onto my soul since that day in the caverns. A truth hammered into bone.

I crushed the thought savagely. Irrelevant. A distraction. A weakness I could *not* afford.

The scent pulled me, hooked into me, leading toward a jagged cluster of boulders bleeding shadow onto the baked ground. Voices drifted on the shimmering air, thin and tense.

"—don't care. We've waited long enough." Vega's voice. Fierce. Stubborn. "Reika said there were others. What if they're stranded in Ignarath territory like she was? What about Kira's sister? We have to—"

"Do you have an actual plan?" Hawk's voice was cool steel layered over something I couldn't name. "Or do you think we can walk in and ask nicely?"

"What do you think?" Vega's voice was getting angrier. "We've heard enough—"

"Rumors get you killed," Hawk shot back. "You're talking about facing winged nightmares without backup."

"Which is why I need you," Vega pressed. "Your eyes. Together—"

"Together we end up trophies on their walls," Hawk snapped. "And do you really think anyone from Scalvaris would try and rescue us?"

I stalked closer, downwind, shadows clinging to me until I could see them. Vega was rigid as a blade. Hawk had her arms crossed, immovable.

"If there's a chance ...," Vega started.

"There isn't." Hawk's word was final, yet something softer underlay it. "Not like this."

"Then come with me. Scout first. Terra doesn't need to know."

The thought of Hawk—*her*—in Ignarath claws ... visions ripped through me. Broken on rocks. Blood staining the dust. Captured. A growl tore low and vicious in my throat, and I struggled to contain it.

"No one is going anywhere." I stepped from the shadows.

They whirled, Hawk's hand blurring toward her hip, Vega dropping into a defensive crouch. Futile. Almost amusing.

"How long have you been eavesdropping?" Hawk demanded, eyes narrowed, chips of ice in the heat.

"Long enough." I advanced, wings flaring just enough to cast them in shadow, to intimidate. "Your mission is over."

Vega's chin lifted. "Wasn't asking permission."

"Obviously." I flashed my fangs. "A stunning display of suicidal stupidity."

"Our people—"

"Are *dead* if they are in Ignarath lands," I cut her off, closing the distance until my shadow consumed her.

She didn't flinch. Admirable idiocy.

"They don't take prisoners. They take pieces. It's a miracle your friend Reika made it out of there."

"We handle ourselves," Vega countered.

"Can you?" My gaze locked onto Hawk, the burning in my chest intensifying, almost like being stabbed. "Do *you* think you can survive what waits out there?"

Calculation flickered in her eyes. Not fear. Awareness. She shrugged. "The ten of us made it here. But if more people crashed on the planet ... we don't know. We owe it to them to try and find out."

That unflinching loyalty struck something deep, a shard of memory—my brother Thrakas, broken, blood on my claws, the weight of failure choking me still.

"Risking everything for ghosts?" I growled, stepping closer to her, drawn by an invisible chain.

"For our people." Her gaze was unwavering. "Wouldn't you?"

The question hit like a physical blow. Yes. I had. And it had cost everything, changed nothing.

Before the words could tear free, a sharp whistle ripped the air.

Alarm.

Instinct slammed down as threat assessment overrode everything.

"Get back to camp," I ordered, the command absolute. "Now."

Vega hesitated, defiance still etched on her face, but Hawk tugged on her arm with a low murmur of, "Later."

I let them pass, my eyes tracking Hawk. The coiled tension in her shoulders, the contained power in her stride. Every line of her screamed strength, resilience, and called to something ancient and savage within me.

Mine.

It wasn't a thought, but a certainty, echoing in the marrow of my bones.

Mine to protect. Mine to claim.

I crushed it again, violently. She was *not* mine. Could not be.

Yet the ache in my fangs grew hotter.

Approaching camp, the threat became sickeningly clear. Five winged shapes tore through the sky, Ignarath silhouettes stark against the blood-streaked sky.

A banner of negotiation—a flimsy shield for their venom—trailed from the leader's spear.

Perfect timing for a disaster.

I shoved past the humans, moving to the center where trainees huddled, a pathetic excuse for a defensive line. Terra stood rigid beside the other humans, watching the descent. If I got Darrokar's mate killed, my life would be forfeit.

And that death would be painful.

I should have never agreed to this mission.

"Hold!" My voice cracked over the camp, silencing nervous whispers. "Look at their banner. We follow protocol, damn them."

The Ignarath circled once—a predator's assessment—then landed, dust puffing up around their claws.

My own claws flexed, aching to grip my sword as I recognized the lead bastard—Plaktish. Scales like poisoned amber, metal bands marking him.

A viper known for smiling while he struck.

"Khorlar Stone Fist." His voice slid smooth as oiled death. "A fortunate encounter."

"Plaktish." My reply was flint. "State your business." We were outside the city but still well within the territory of Scalvaris. These interlopers had no reason to be there.

Not unless they wanted to cause trouble.

His smile widened, all fangs. "Direct. Charming."

His gaze slid over the camp, lingering on the humans like a scavenger eyeing fresh kills. "I represent my High Council. Seeking ... resolution ... for recent troubles."

Silence. Let him spit his poison.

"Three patrols attacked." Plaktish purred the words. "Our warriors dead. Weapons gone." His eyes hardened, chips of obsidian. "The survivors described Scalvaris attackers."

"Impossible," I snapped.

Plaktish's smile stretched, predatory. "A flat denial? How interesting."

A trap. Baited and set. I tasted ash.

"What do you want?" I demanded, shedding the pretense of diplomacy like scorched scales.

He flared his wings slightly, a calculated display. "We demand a blood price. It's tradition."

"Bring evidence to Darrokar if you believe Scalvaris warriors were involved." My voice was flat stone. "This isn't the place."

"Oh, but it is." His gaze drifted, deliberate, snagging on Hawk. "We are happy to take your humans as payment."

A lightning strike of rage. Hot. Blinding.

A growl tore free from my deepest chest, raw and uncontrolled. My wings flared wide, muscles bunched, stepping forward without thought. Blind, primal fury—utterly beyond my control.

For *her*.

"You will take *nothing*." I snarled the words, fangs bared, the world narrowing to him, to the threat.

Plaktish's gaze didn't waver, but a flicker of calculation showed. He saw it. Saw the crack in my control.

Dangerous. I'd shown too much.

"Careful, Stone Fist." His voice dropped, laced with menace. "We wouldn't want hostilities."

2

HAWK

BAD. This was volcanic eruption inside a crashing spaceship bad.

The air didn't just crackle—it felt thick enough to choke on, heavy with the heat rolling off the cracked earth and the sudden, predatory weight that slammed down with Plaktish's words.

We'll take your humans as payment.

Audacity wasn't a strong enough word. It was a physical blow, stealing the air from my lungs, leaving a ringing silence behind the raw demand.

Beside me, Vega was a live wire. I didn't just see her rage; I felt it humming off her skin, a dangerous vibration that tightened the knot already forming low in my gut. Her knuckles were bone-white on the hilt of the knife she gripped, her whole body coiled so tight I swear I could hear the scream building in her throat.

She was going to launch herself—her stupid, loyal, suicidal self—straight into those Ignarath claws. And then some of us were going to die. Including me, since my stupid ass was going to have to defend her.

But before the thought fully formed, before Vega could explode, something shifted. A pressure change. A wall of granite-gray muscle didn't just move—it *materialized* between us and the sneering Ignarath leader.

Khorlar.

A blur of shadow and scale, faster than anything that massive had a right to be, planting himself like a mountain. His wings flared—a ripple of dark membrane—but it was enough. Enough to cast a shadow that felt suddenly cold despite the twin suns beating down.

My own hand spasmed, fingers brushing the familiar hardness of the knife at my thigh. What I wouldn't do for a blaster. Or a gun.

Around us, the air vibrated. Drakarn trainees shifted, the scrape of claws on scorched rock impossibly loud in the sudden quiet, weapons half-drawn despite Plaktish's flimsy negotiation flag. Across the clearing, Terra's eyes met mine—a grim, silent warning: *hold*.

My gaze locked on Khorlar, narrowed, dissecting. Every survival instinct screamed *danger*. The Drakarn were powerful. Alien. In the months since we'd crashed on Scalvaris, I kept thinking I was used to them. And then ...

Yeah, there was no getting used to seven-foot-tall dragon men. And Khorlar was taller than most. Bigger than most. I tried to tell my body that was scary and not sexy.

And now was *not* the time for that argument.

What had he thought when he overheard Vega's plans? What would he *do*? She was getting more reckless, desperate. I was afraid she was going to act alone if one of us didn't find a way to make her see sense. And if it came down to the Drakarn knocking that sense into her?

She was screwed.

But watching him now ... immovable, radiating a fury so contained it felt like it might crack the air around him ... something else stirred. Not trust. But a grudging ... acknowledgment? Recognition? The sheer, overwhelming force was, for once, pointed *away* from us.

And that growl. The one that had ripped from

his chest when Plaktish made his demand. It hadn't been calculated. It had been torn from somewhere deep, somewhere primal. Possessive. The sound had vibrated low, not just in the air, but somewhere deep in *my* own bones.

And, well, other places. Places that had no right to be acknowledged on the battlefield.

Khorlar wanted to protect us. *Me*—Plaktish's gaze had snagged on me, oily and appraising, right before he spoke. The realization sent a bizarre, cold trickle down my spine, chased by an unwanted flush of heat.

"You will take *nothing*," Khorlar snarled again, the words less spoken, more carved into the charged air. Low. Menacing. His fangs were fully bared now, wickedly sharp. The heat radiating off him wasn't just the planet; it was focused rage.

Plaktish didn't flinch, but his greasy smile stretched tighter, thinning his lips. I saw it—the flicker of calculation in those yellow eyes. He'd prodded the stone beast and gotten a tremor he hadn't banked on. He saw the crack in the granite control.

"Careful, Stone Fist," Plaktish purred, the sound like oil sliding over gravel, meant to unnerve. "Hostilities would be ... unfortunate. I am proposing a simple solution."

"Demanding another clan's people ...," Khorlar bit out the word *people* like it tasted strange, "is not a solution. It is insult."

Each syllable was flint striking steel. He surged forward another half-step, crowding Plaktish, the sheer difference in their bulk suddenly overwhelming. Beside his comrades, Plaktish was overwhelming. Next to Khorlar, he looked almost small. "You have no claim. No evidence. Take your accusations to Scalvaris. Appeal to the Blade Council. If you *dare*."

My breath caught in my throat. I could almost picture what would happen if this went wrong—Plaktish calling the bluff, the roar, the clash. Vega was practically vibrating beside me now, radiating pure kill-intent. My hand clamped firmly down on her arm. A silent, desperate *hold*.

We had the numbers, but most of the Drakarn with us were trainees, and new trainees at that. A fight now could not go well.

Shockingly, Plaktish hesitated. His gaze flickered —Khorlar's immovable presence, the wary readiness of the trainees, the small knot of human women armed with knives and sheer, stubborn fury. Weighing the odds.

A fight here? Against Khorlar? Not a sure thing. Provoking Scalvaris without solid proof? Bad politics, even for an Ignarath snake.

I wasn't positive of the dynamics. This was so far from Earth. But people were people, even when they weren't human.

The slimy smile resurfaced, colder this time, dead in the eyes. "Very well, Stone Fist. Your ... *protectiveness* ... is noted." He spat the word like poison. "We *will* appeal. The High Council expects satisfaction."

One last look swept over us—over *me*.

It felt like something crawling under my training leathers, leaving a trail of slime. My fingers *ached* for my gun, a sharp, physical yearning to wipe that look off his face. I forced my hand open, palm sweating, forced my breathing into a semblance of evenness.

Reaction equals death. But the image ... oh, the image was satisfying.

With sharp, angry beats of powerful wings, the Ignarath launched themselves upward, kicking dust and grit into our faces. Five dark silhouettes against the blinding double suns. They circled once—a final, contemptuous assessment—then banked sharply, heading for the jagged silhouette of the cliffs etched against the horizon.

The tension didn't break. It just ... shifted. Became something heavier, colder.

"Break camp!" Khorlar's voice wasn't just a command; it was a physical force, shattering the brittle silence. Absolute. No room for anything but obedience.

He pivoted, his dark gaze sweeping over the trainees, then snagging on us. On me. "We return to Scalvaris. *Now*." He stabbed a thick, clawed finger at a younger Drakarn, her scales like polished night. "Bryshe! Fly ahead. Warn the Council. An Ignarath delegation approaches. They're claiming raids. Demanding recompense." He paused, his voice dropping, hardening. "They want the humans."

Bryshe nodded. Then she launched herself skyward, a powerful downbeat of wings catching a thermal, soaring away with a grace that punched me right in the chest.

I watched her go, my eyes tracking her ascent until she was a disappearing speck against the harsh, unforgiving glare.

And the ache hit me. Physical. A hollow space under my ribs, a phantom weight in my hands that should have been a flight stick. God, the *sky*.

Rushing past, the world tilting below, the sheer *freedom* of it. Missing it felt like missing a limb, a constant, dull throb under the surface of everything.

Being grounded here ... it was like being buried alive.

But there were no planes on Scalvaris. No gliders. No way to take to the sky if you weren't born with wings.

I shook my head, forcing the feeling down, locking it away. No time. Checklist. Water. Rations. Medkit. Knife secure? Yes. Survival mode engaged. Automatic. Efficient.

I knelt, hands moving mechanically, securing the straps on my pack. Keep busy. Don't think.

Don't *feel*.

Then a shadow fell over me.

My muscles went rigid. Every nerve ending screamed. I didn't need to look. The sheer *presence* was enough, a weight pressing down on the air. And the scent ... faint, almost scrubbed clean by the wind, but there.

Ozone and hot stone. Khorlar.

Was this it? The dressing down? The warning about Vega? About the Ignarath looking at me like a piece of meat? His face, when I finally risked a glance up, was carved granite. Unreadable. As always.

He didn't speak. Just stood there. Watching me. The silence stretched, thin and tight. Then, he bent, a slow, deliberate movement, his massive frame blocking the harsh sunlight. His clawed hand reached down.

My own hand flew to my knife hilt. Pure reflex. As if I had a shot against a monster like him. My heart hammered against my ribs, a frantic bird trapped in a cage.

But he wasn't attacking. His claws—sharp, scarred, lethally practical—closed around something small and metallic glinting in the dust near my boot. My multi-tool. It must have fallen.

Without a word, he straightened and held it out.

His hand hung in the air between us. Large. Rough-scaled. Warmth radiated from it, surprisingly intense. The gesture was ... nothing. Simple. Neutral. Just my tool, held steady.

My breath hitched. Hesitantly, numbly, I reached out. My fingers brushed against his scales. Rougher than they looked. And hot. Like stone left under a desert sun. A tiny shock, sharp and distinct, jumped between us. Static electricity. Had to be.

His eyes—yellow depths, slitted pupils

narrowing slightly—met mine. Just for a second. An eternity. Nothing readable there. Utterly alien.

Then he straightened fully, turned without a sound, and stalked away to bark orders at the trainees.

Leaving me kneeling in the dust, multi-tool clutched tight in my suddenly trembling hand, the ghost of that warmth, that unexpected jolt, still singing under my skin.

He hadn't yelled. He hadn't threatened. He'd just ... picked up my tool.

What in the seven hells was *that?*

The ground felt unsteady beneath my knees. The distrust was still there, cold and hard in my gut. But now ... now it had company. A swirling, confusing eddy of ... something else. Something I didn't have a name for.

God damn it, this couldn't be good.

3

KHORLAR

THE BLADE COUNCIL chambers devoured sound like a starving predator ate its bloodied prey, the ancient stone drinking in every whisper until only the thundering of my pulse remained in my ears. Obsidian pillars stretched toward the vaulted ceiling where light from heat crystals pierced the gloom.

I stood rigid. Claws flexing. Every muscle coiled tight with the effort of restraint. The Council sat in their carved stone seats, a half-circle of Scalvaris's finest warriors, their faces carved from the same unforgiving rock as the chamber itself.

Darrokar's obsidian scales caught the sparse light, crimson undertones pulsing with each measured breath.

Beside him sat Terra, his human mate who had somehow earned her place at his side. Her face betrayed nothing, but the slight tension in her shoulders spoke volumes. She understood what was at stake.

The Ignarath hadn't come for peace.

They'd come to test our weaknesses.

And they'd brought an audience.

My nostrils flared at the unexpected scent of sacred oils—Karyseth, High Priestess of the Forge Temple, her silver-streaked scales gleaming, flanked by three silent, yellow robed acolytes. Their presence made my scales itch. The Temple rarely involved itself in Council matters unless blood or blades were involved. But in the past year, things had changed.

They sensed weakness. And the temple wanted power.

Plaktish prowled the center of the chamber, his posture a calculated insult to every warrior present, his scales catching the light like poisoned honey. Four Ignarath warriors flanked him, each bearing ceremonial arms—another insult veiled as tradition. His smile was all fangs, his eyes cold and calculating as they swept over us.

"We appreciate Scalvaris's prompt response to our ... concerns." His voice slithered through the chamber. "The High Council of Ignarath values our tenuous peace."

"State your grievance." Darrokar's low rumble cut through the pretense.

A flash of irritation crossed Plaktish's features before the mask slipped back into place. He gestured sharply.

One of his warriors stepped forward, unrolling a blood-stained cloth.

Six Ignarath battle talons. Severed at the joint.

"Six scouts." Plaktish's voice hardened. "Slaughtered in our territory. Mutilated."

Murmurs rippled through the Council. I remained stone-still, watching. There was always violence in the Western Crags—contested land where blood had been spilled for generations. Then again, I looked sidelong at Vyne, who was scowling at the delegation.

A few weeks ago, he and his now mate, Selene, had secretly journeyed to the Harrovan Mountains in Ignarath territory to retrieve a plant to heal the sick. And they had dealt with Ignarath scouts. I'd been there to see some of it.

"And you claim Scalvaris warriors are responsible?" Zarvash leaned forward, his bronze scales catching the light.

"The survivors described the attackers clearly." Plaktish's gaze swept the chamber, finally landing on me. "Drakarn with the distinctive battle markings of Scalvaris. They even described a warrior bearing the Stone Fist emblem."

My blood froze. A direct accusation.

"Impossible." The word tore from my throat, rough-edged and dangerous. "I do not slaughter sleeping enemies."

And when attacked, I did not leave survivors to tell tales.

Plaktish's smile widened fractionally. "Yet here we stand, with six dead and witnesses who say otherwise." He turned back to Darrokar. "The High Council demands reparations. Blood for blood."

Darrokar's wings shifted slightly—the only outward sign of his tension. "What evidence beyond this do you bring? Battle talons prove deaths, not murder."

"Would you like us to bring the survivors to testify?" Plaktish countered. "They are prepared to swear on the Sacred Flame that they recognized Scalvaris warriors."

Karyseth stepped forward then, her ceremonial robes whispering against the stone floor. "The

Temple would witness such an oath," she said, her voice like ancient stone.

Plaktish hesitated—barely a flicker, but I caught it. A sworn testimony before the Forge Priestess would be binding. False claims would mean punishment from the Temple itself.

"That will not be necessary at this stage," he recovered quickly.

Of course. His witnesses would crumble under the Temple's scrutiny. But why was he lying at all? It was true that Vyne and I had dispatched with Ignarath scouts, but with the rogues in the area, it would be impossible to prove. Still, he could try.

So why the ruse?

"What reparations do you seek?" Terra's voice cut through the tension, sharp as a blade.

Plaktish's gaze shifted to her, lingering a moment too long.

"Ah, the human voice of reason." His tone made my claws itch to tear into his throat. "Ignarath proposes a simple exchange."

"Explain." Darrokar's command was granite.

"We wish to know how many human slaves Scalvaris harbors. And we will take our fair share." Plaktish's eyes glittered with naked greed. "And we wish to ... study them. Their abilities. Their technology."

The pieces locked into place. This wasn't about dead scouts. This was about the humans. About knowledge and power and the advantage they represented.

"Very well," said Darrokar, and a growl threatened to escape my throat before he continued. "We harbor no human slaves." Darrokar's voice dropped to a dangerous register that made even the stone beneath our feet seem to tremble.

"Do you call them citizens?" Plaktish's laugh was cold. "Allies? We've heard rumors of your strange ... attachment ..." He gestured toward Terra. "But surely you can't claim them all."

"The humans choose their own path," Darrokar replied. "They are free, not property."

"Free?" Plaktish's gaze swept the chamber, settling finally on me. "Is that what you call them, Stone Fist? I noticed your ... fierce defense ... of one particular human during our encounter. The dark-skinned female with the short hair." His smile turned predatory. "Is she yours?"

The question hit me right between the ribs.

Heat surged through my body, a molten wave that threatened to consume all reason. My fangs throbbed with a searing pain that radiated deep into my skull. Hawk's face flashed in my mind—her fierce eyes, the defiant set of her jaw, the way she moved like a predator despite her fragile human form.

Her scent. Gods, her scent haunted me even now, a phantom that teased at the edges of my awareness.

"Yes."

The word escaped before I could cage it, raw and absolute, echoing through the suddenly silent chamber.

Mine.

The word burned through my consciousness, bypassing reason, strategy, duty.

Mine.

Not a thought but a certainty carved into my bones.

Stunned silence crashed down. I felt the weight of every stare—Darrokar's sharp assessment, Terra's widened eyes, the Council's collective shock.

Even Karyseth stepped forward, her ancient eyes narrowing with sudden interest.

The admission burned in my throat like molten steel, undeniable and irreversible. I had never intended to claim her, to acknowledge the pull that had been tormenting me since I first caught her scent. Yet the thought of Plaktish's oily gaze upon her, the idea that she could be traded away like a weapon or a trinket ...

My control had shattered like brittle stone.

"Interesting." Plaktish's voice dripped with satisfaction. He'd gotten exactly what he wanted—information. "I wasn't aware Scalvaris had formalized bonds with the humans. How many others have been ... claimed?"

"That is not your concern," Darrokar cut in, his voice a sharp edge.

"When it affects the balance of power on Volcaryth, it becomes everyone's concern," Plaktish countered. "Ignarath merely wishes to understand our ... changing world."

"You wish to exploit it," I growled. "Your accusations of raids are fabricated to justify your demands."

Plaktish's eyes hardened. "Strong words, Stone Fist. Would you call me a liar before your Council and the Temple?"

"I call you what you are," I replied, my voice steady despite the storm raging within. "A scavenger picking at wounds you hope to widen."

Karyseth's ceremonial staff struck the stone floor with a sound like thunder. "The Temple takes note of these accusations." Her ancient voice commanded attention. "If blood has truly been spilled as claimed, the Sacred Flame demands proper rites and true accounting." She turned her gaze to Plaktish. "The Ignarath witnesses will present themselves at the Temple for truthspeaking."

Plaktish's composure cracked. Truthspeaking before the priestesses was no small matter. Lies told under their rituals resulted in consequences few survived.

"The witnesses have suffered enough trauma," he demurred. "Perhaps another solution—"

"No." Darrokar rose to his full height, wings partially extended in a display of dominance. "There will be no reparations without truth. Either your witnesses appear before the Temple, or your claims are dismissed."

The chamber filled with the low rumble of Council approval. Plaktish's eyes narrowed, calculation evident in every line of his body.

"Very well," he conceded with false grace. "I will convey your ... requirements ... to the High Council. But know this: The humans change everything. Their presence upsets balances that have existed for generations. Scalvaris cannot hoard such power without consequences."

Darrokar signaled to the chamber guards. "You have delivered your message."

Plaktish bowed—the precise degree that conveyed respect while implying none—and turned to leave with his warriors. As he passed me, he paused, his voice pitched for my ears alone. "She must be quite remarkable, Stone Fist, to crack your legendary control. I look forward to meeting her properly."

My growl erupted from depths I rarely accessed —a promise of violence so explicit that even Plaktish stepped back.

"You will never touch her."

"I SWEAR to whatever gods this hellhole has, if one more oversized lizard tells me 'it's for our protection,' I'm going to start removing scales with my bare hands!"

Vega's voice slammed off the stone walls of our new "accommodations"—a glorified bunker carved deep into the heart of Scalvaris. Bigger, yes. Higher ceilings, multiple chambers. It still felt like a cage. The air, thick and recycled, pressed in.

Nobody was taking it well. The tension was a physical thing, a knot tightening low in my back, pulling my shoulders taut.

"I knew this would happen," Reika whispered, her voice thin and brittle. She paced the perimeter like a trapped animal, fingers ghosting over the rough stone, searching for an escape hatch that wasn't there. Escaping Ignarath territory only to be confined again ... it had scraped something bloody inside her. "They're going to kill us."

"We're not trapped," I said, forcing steadiness into my voice, fighting the tremor that wanted to betray the exhaustion clawing at me. "The door isn't locked. It's guarded. Against the Ignarath." My own words sounded hollow.

"Same difference," Vega snapped, her fist cracking against the wall. Boom. The sound ricocheted off the stone, up my legs, making my teeth ache. Frustration made tangible. "They're controlling us either way."

Kira stood near an air shaft, crystal-lined and narrow, her face a mask of calm that didn't fool me for a second. I knew that stillness. Knew the storm gathering beneath. "We need to stop just ... going along," she said, her voice dangerously quiet. "What if my sister is with them? With the Ignarath?"

My stomach didn't just drop. It plummeted, a sickening lurch like hitting zero-G without warning. Cold dread blooming. "Kira—"

"They mentioned other humans," she pressed, voice hardening into that detached planning mode that always preceded something drastic. "What if

Larissa is *there*? Held by them? And we're just sitting here? Waiting?"

Eden huddled near Kaiya, eyes wide, absorbing the rising panic. Reika kept pacing, offering nothing. Weeks there, and she still hadn't shared what she saw, what the Ignarath did to humans.

We were fracturing. I could feel the pressure building, hairline cracks spreading through our forced unity. The air felt charged, heavy with unspoken fear, a thing I could almost taste—metallic, like blood.

"Enough!" The word ripped from my throat, rougher than I intended, louder than I expected. Command presence, Academy training—all fraying at the edges.

Every head snapped toward me. Defiance, fear, desperate hope—reflected back, a weight pressing down, heavy as planetary gravity. Terra was gone, summoned by Darrokar. That meant that leadership defaulted to me.

I didn't ask for it. Didn't want it. But there we were.

"Look," I tried again, forcing my tone softer, gentler. "I get it. This sucks. More than sucks. But charging out half-cocked? That's chaos. Division. It's exactly what the Ignarath want." I met Vega's glare. "We have to be smarter."

"So we just sit here?" Vega challenged, though the fire in her voice had banked slightly, replaced by a weary frustration.

I shook my head, feeling the grit of Scalvaris dust in my hair. "We plan. We survive." My gaze found Kira's, desperate and intense. "And we don't give up on Larissa. Or anyone else. But we do this *right*."

"And what's right?" Kira whispered, the question hanging, sharp and pointed.

Before I could even think to form an answer, the heavy stone door groaned open. Every muscle in the room went rigid. I moved automatically, stepping forward, putting myself between them and whatever was coming.

Khorlar was what was coming.

Filling the doorway like a living mountain carved from granite. His scales drank the dim light. Wings folded tight, but their sheer bulk dominated the space. His golden eyes swept the room in cold assessment before locking onto me.

An unwelcome jolt, sharp and electric, shot through me. Not just awareness. Something hotter. Something invasive that coiled low and tight in my belly, a sickening warmth I fought to ignore.

I hated it. Hated the feeling, hated the loss of control, hated that *he* could evoke it.

"Sarah Hawkins," he rumbled. That voice. Deep, graveled, bypassing my ears to vibrate somewhere deep in my bones.

"It's Hawk," I snapped. My pulse hammered against my ribs like something was trying to bash its way out. "What now?"

His expression didn't change, but something flickered in those predator eyes—a flash of heat, instantly smothered. "You will come with me."

Dead silence. My own heartbeat roared in my ears.

"Like hell she will," Vega snarled, moving up beside me, hand dropping instinctively to her knife hilt.

Khorlar didn't glance her way. His gaze stayed pinned on me. Unwavering. Expectant. As if my agreement was inevitable.

As if I was already his.

Heat flared under my skin. Anger. It had to be anger. What else could it be? "Whatever you need to say, say it here." My voice was tight. "I'm not leaving them."

"This is not a request," he replied, each word carved from granite.

"And that's not an answer."

Something dangerous crossed his face then—not just anger, something older, more primal—gone as quickly as it appeared. "The Ignarath have taken a ... particular interest in you. You require additional security measures."

Ice formed in my gut, twisting tighter. Plaktish. His oily stare sliding over me in the desert. The flick of his tongue tasting the air near my skin. My stomach churned at the memory.

But why *me*?

"All the more reason to stay with my people," I argued, gesturing behind me. "Safety in numbers."

"Your presence endangers them," Khorlar stated, blunt as a hammer blow. "If the Ignarath target this location seeking you, they will harm anyone in their path."

The air punched from my lungs. I glanced back. Reika's pale face. Kira's clenched jaw. Eden's terrified eyes. Bringing danger down on them ... the thought was a physical weight.

"Bullshit," Vega hissed. "We stick together. Always."

Everything in me screamed agreement. Stay. Keep us whole. But his logic, cold and sharp, cut through the sentiment. If I was the target ...

"Hawk," Kira said softly, her analytical mind already there. "Maybe ... maybe he's right."

"I just got them calm," I muttered, just loud enough so she could hear.

"And they'll unravel if you fight the dragon-guard," she countered, just as quiet. "If you *are* the target ..."

I squeezed my eyes shut, hating the logic. Couldn't refute it. I opened my eyes to find Khorlar watching, nostrils flaring just a little, that unsettling intensity focused entirely on me. He was scenting me. Tasting the air between us like ... like prey? No, something else. Something that made my own breath catch.

"Fine," I said finally, the word scraping like gravel from my throat. "But I want daily updates. Full reports."

A single, curt nod from Khorlar.

"You can't be serious." Vega grabbed my arm, fingers digging in, desperate. "We don't split up. Rule one."

I turned to her, forcing my voice to steady, locking my knees against a sudden tremble. "I need you here, Vega. They need you. Terra's gone, Orla and Selene are with their mates. I need someone strong watching their backs. Can you do that?"

Cheap manipulation. Appealing to her fierce protectiveness. But I needed compliance, not approval. Her jaw worked, the internal battle visible. Finally, a sharp, jerky nod.

"You check in," she ordered. "Or I'm coming for you, scales be damned."

"Fair enough." I squeezed her shoulder, then faced the others. "Stay smart. Stay together. I'll be back." The fear in their eyes nearly broke me. Crash landing, survival, negotiation ... we'd forged something strong in that fire. This felt like ripping off a limb.

But the decision was made. "Lead the way."

He turned without a word, filling the corridor. I followed, matching his long strides, refusing to scurry. Thighs burning, but pride wouldn't let me falter.

Was this how Terra felt all those months ago? Dragged away by Darrokar? Not that Khorlar was claiming me ... but the echo was disturbing.

Deeper into the mountain city. Winding passages spiraling down. Cooler air, thick with mineral scents coating my tongue. There were fewer Drakarn here. The ones we passed nodded deferentially to Khorlar, eyes sliding to me, filled with open curiosity.

"Where exactly are we going?" My voice echoed strangely. Minutes of silence stretched thin.

"Siege quarters," he replied, not looking back.

"You think we're under siege already?"

"Preparation is not paranoia."

I rolled my eyes at his rigid back, the tightly folded wings. "Pretty sure paranoid people say that exact thing."

No verbal response, but tension tightened his shoulders. Wings shifted. A tiny ripple. It struck a nerve. Good.

An archway carved with battle scenes—Drakarn warriors, wings spread, claws tearing into enemies. Beyond it, a massive circular chamber, doorways radiating out. High ceiling, dotted with heat crystals casting a warm, intimate-yet-exposed glow.

He stopped at one door and revealed a spacious chamber. "This is where you will stay," he stated, gesturing me inside.

My steps were cautious as I gave the room a quick scan. Spartan was generous. A stone platform with silks—a bed. Bathing alcove. A simple table, two stone chairs.

Bare walls. Utilitarian. Cold.

But the air ... warmer than the corridor. And carrying a faint musk. Not unpleasant. His scent.

There was a jolt low in my stomach. He'd been there. Recently.

"Wow," I drawled, dropping my pack with a precise thud. Echoed loudly. "Love what you've done with the place. Really screams 'Khorlar.'"

His brow ridge furrowed. "These are not my personal quarters."

"You could've fooled me. The total lack of anything remotely welcoming? Definitely your style."

Irritation? Close. A muscle twitched in his jaw. His wings rustled like disturbed leather. "These are siege chambers. They are built for function, not comfort."

"And your actual quarters?" Curiosity, sharp and unwelcome, pricked at me.

"Council members maintain private chambers here during times of crisis."

Not an answer. Typical.

"Lucky me," I muttered, circling the room again. Boots scraped on stone. I turned to face him and planted my feet. "Are you going to tell me what's *really* going on? Why me? Why the sudden Ignarath obsession?"

There was that predatory stillness. Utterly alien despite the almost humanoid shape. His eyes tracked me, pupils narrowing. The weight of his gaze was physical, sliding over my skin, raising gooseflesh I fought to suppress.

"Plaktish identified you as a target," he said finally, a low rumble.

"I got that part. Why *me?* Not Terra? Not Vega?" I crossed my arms. It was a defensive posture. Shielding myself from that stare as much as projecting defiance.

A flicker across his face. Too fast to read. Discomfort? Hesitation? His nostrils flared again. He was tasting the air. Tasting *me.* My skin prickled with heat that had nothing to do with the warm temperature.

"Terra is Darrokar's mate. Protected." His words were measured. Too careful. "You were observed. During the training exercise. Your skills ..."

A harsh snort escaped me. Unladylike. I didn't care. "Bullshit. We all have skills. There's more."

His jaw tightened. That muscle worked again beneath the scales. Wings shifted, spreading slightly, then folding tight. Agitation. A tell. "It is ... complicated."

"Uncomplicate it." My heart was hammering a frantic rhythm against my ribs. Could he hear it? "I'm isolated. Dragged down here. I deserve the whole truth."

His wings rippled again. A subtle shift of membrane catching low light. His gaze flickered around the room, then snapped back to me. Unnerving intensity. Prickling heat crawling over my skin.

"The Ignarath seek leverage," he stated, the words heavy. "They may believe you hold ... value."

"To whom?" I pressed, stepping closer despite the warning bells screaming in my head. His scent intensified—hot stone, wild spice. It made my head spin. "To Terra? Darrokar? Scalvaris?"

His nostrils flared. Wide, then narrow, a slow inhalation. He was scenting me again. A shiver traced its way down my spine, involuntary and infuriating.

"To me," he said. The words dropped like stones into silence.

I blinked, thrown. Mouth dry. Then watering. "What are you talking about?"

"During the Council meeting. Plaktish ...," Khorlar's voice deepened into something darker. "made insinuations. About you." He hesitated. "He suggested you might be ... claimed."

Claimed. The word hung there. Heavy. Loaded

with implications I didn't want to understand. My chest tightened, breath caught.

"Claimed," I repeated flatly. The word tasted like ash. "Like ... property?"

A low growl rumbled from his chest, vibrating through the stone floor, up my legs, settling in my bones. A physical force. "No. Not property."

"Then what?" I demanded, frustration building, pressing behind my eyes. "Because this feels damn close! Moved around, isolated, 'protected' whether I want it or not!"

"It is not—" He cut himself off, visibly struggling. His claws flexed at his sides. They were deadly, beautiful. Alien. His voice was more controlled when he spoke again. Measured. "The Ignarath *believe* you hold significance to me. They would use that perception."

The pieces slammed together in my head, sharp edges grinding. Leverage? Using *me*? Heat flooded my face, stinging my cheeks. Anger, pure and sharp. "What. Did. You. Do?"

His expression remained stone, but his eyes ... a flash of defiance? Regret? Something deeper that clenched my stomach with an emotion I refused to name.

"What was necessary," he said simply.

"Necessary?" The word echoed, bouncing off the stone, twisted. "Necessary for *what*? To mark your territory? What the hell happened in that meeting?"

First Darrokar, now him. Was this some alien mating ritual bullshit again?

"There was no time for consultation." His tone hardened, wings spreading slightly. Unconscious display of dominance. Making himself bigger. "Plaktish intended to take you. To Ignarath."

"So you decided to 'claim' me instead," I stated, bitterness sharp on my tongue. "How is that any different?"

"I did *not* claim you," Khorlar growled, the sound vibrating through me. His wings flared wider, webbing flushing darker. Heat? Anger? Something else? "I *prevented* them from taking you."

"By saying I was yours," I shot back. Heart pounding, a frantic drumbeat—rage, confusion, and that other thing. That damn heat making my skin feel too tight.

"By stating you were under my protection," he corrected, eyes darkening, amber turning to burnished, terrifying gold.

Deep breath. Steady. Try to steady. This was ... too much.

And one glaring issue remained. My eyes

snagged on the sleeping platform, large enough for ... two? A sudden, suffocating tightness gripped my chest. "One bed," I stated flatly, the words clipped. Don't look at it. "Was *that* part of your grand protection strategy?"

His gaze followed mine, then snapped back to my face. Pupils dilated, then contracted to slits. "Yes." A beat. He cleared his throat. "No. There was no time ... for servants to rearrange."

That first syllable. Yes. Neutral, yet loaded. Sent fresh heat crawling over my skin. "Well, that's not happening," I stated firmly, eyes locked on his, refusing to glance back at the bed. "Ground rules. If I'm stuck here."

His brow ridge lifted. Silent. Waiting. The intensity of his focus was unnerving. A predator deciding.

"One," I began, ticking fingers off. Hands steady, thank god. Insides churning. Talking too fast, need to control this. "I'm not sharing that bed."

"Two, no touching. Not unless I'm literally about to be skewered. Three—" I stepped closer, invading his space, forcing him to look down at me. Close enough to see the gold flecks swirling in his irises. Close enough for his heat to radiate against my skin. "You tell me *everything*. No half-truths. No convenient omissions. I need the whole damn picture."

He regarded me silently. Long moments stretched. The air thickened, suddenly heavy, charged with static ... or something else. Something I refused to name. His scent—that impossible mix of hot stone and wild spice—wrapped around me, coiling in my lungs. My head spun. And my mouth ... my mouth watered. A bizarre, unnerving reaction that had nothing to do with fear and everything to do with the predator standing too close.

Finally, a slight inclination of his head. "Acceptable terms."

"Good." Some tension eased from my shoulders, immediately replaced by a new, prickling awareness. "Now. Where are *you* sleeping?"

"The floor will suffice." He paused, gaze sweeping the room, then returning to me. "If I am to protect you—and you *do* require protection," he added, cutting off my objection before it formed, "then I must remain. In this room. On this, I must insist."

"Perfect." No sympathy. He made this bed ... or rather, this situation. I grabbed my pack, exhaustion hitting me like a physical blow. Emotional whiplash. Limbs heavy. Thoughts sluggish. "I'm resting. Long day."

Khorlar nodded once. Paused in the doorway,

silhouetted. Light caught his scales, shifting gray to silver.

"Sarah," he said, using my name again. That careful tone tightening my chest.

"Hawk," I corrected, automatic, weary.

"Hawk," he acknowledged. "You are not claimed. You are not property. But you *are* protected." His eyes locked with mine, molten gold holding me captive. I felt the heat of his gaze like a physical touch, unwanted, unsettling. "Do not mistake one for the other."

The words hung there, a promise and a threat, stirring that damned treacherous warmth deep inside me all over again.

5

KHORLAR

TWO DAYS.

A lifetime trapped in shared quarters. Her scent —alien sweetness, sharp and clinging—wasn't just in the air. It had burrowed *under* my scales, sunk into the ancient stone, woven itself through the stifling silence between us.

I spent two days watching her move. She had quick, contained energy. A predator penned. Each clipped step was a friction against my fraying restraint. Her voice rang deep in my bones. It clawed its way inside and took root where I couldn't dig it out.

Two days. And the lies piled between us like a slag heap, heavy and foul.

The stone floor offered no peace beneath my back through the endless, watchful nights.

Sleep?

It was a forgotten luxury. Darkness only sharpened it all. The whisper-rustle of silk as she shifted on her sleeping platform. The soft huff of her breath across the chamber. *Her.* Her nearness was a physical pressure. A brand against my senses.

Mine.

The word wasn't a thought. It was a blood-beat. A marrow-deep certainty. My fangs *throbbed*—not a dull ache, but a searing, insistent pulse keeping rhythm with her breathing. It was a fire smoldering behind my eyes.

I had claimed her before the Blade Council, the Temple, Plaktish. A public declaration, witnessed by the Old Bloods.

But not to *her.*

The deception coiled, cold and scaled in my gut. Was it necessary? Protective? The excuses were thin as cooled lava crust, cracking under the weight of truth. She didn't understand. *Couldn't* understand the primal power in her scent, a call threatening to shatter hard earned Drakarn control, tradition, *everything.*

So I lied. I used omission and misdirection. I let her believe this was protection. Politics. Nothing more.

Ash and lies.

I watched her prepare for the day. She moved with ritualistic efficiency. She laced worn boots tight. She checked the knife at her hip—always the knife, loose in its sheath, ready. That close-cropped hair, dark as volcanic glass, was smoothed back with quick, practiced swipes. Her skin caught the glow from the heat crystals, a rich and warm brown compared to my own ridged, gray hide.

She looked up. Caught me watching her. Her eyes narrowed—not fear. Never fear with her. She showed calculation. A challenge simmered just below the surface.

"Staring again, Stone Fist." Her voice was low, cutting. She used the old warrior name.

Was it deliberate provocation?

I didn't deny it. I couldn't seem to look away. "Duties," I grated instead, the word rough, ill-fitting in the charged air.

"Then let's move." She straightened. All coiled muscle and lethal grace. "No more cage. I'm going with you today, Khorlar, or I find my own way back."

My wings stirred against my back, involuntary. The membranes tightened like drum skin. "That is unwise."

News of my claim had no doubt rung out

through the city. If we were observed, there would be ... expectations. Expectations I could not meet with the rules my Hawk had given me.

"So is ignorance." She stepped closer. Fearless. Too close. My chest tightened, a painful clench around my core. Her scent spiked—that clean, sharp sweetness fogging my thoughts, clouding judgment. "I'm going stir-crazy in here, Khorlar."

My name. The curve of her lips around the syllables sent a jolt straight through me. It was primal, an ancient hunger that stirred deep in my mind's bedrock. *Control.* I was losing this battle. Had been losing it since the moment I'd pulled her from the falling rock, felt her impossible warmth, a shock against my scales.

"Very well," I conceded, the words forced past the constriction in my throat. They were raw-edged. "But you stay close. No wandering."

A ghost of a smile flickered across her face. It was rare. Transforming. It hooked something vital inside me, pulling tight. "Deal."

Central Scalvaris seemed more crowded than usual. Warriors were heading for the training caverns, their scales gleaming dully. Craftsmen hauled geodes and obsidian shards. Merchants hawked spiced meats and woven fire-grass near the banks of the river. It was a familiar rhythm. Now jarring. With *her* beside me.

Conversations choked mid-word as we passed. Gazes snagged on Hawk, then skittered away when they met mine. Space opened around us. A sudden vacuum in the crowd. Each reaction was a hammer blow against my composure. *Claimed.* They knew. Everyone knew.

She didn't.

Hawk noticed. Of course, she did. Those sharp eyes missed nothing. She was cataloguing the whispers, the averted faces, the sudden tension thick as geyser steam.

"Problem?" she asked, a low murmur, pitched only for my ears. "Or does everyone usually flinch when the great Stone Fist walks by?"

"They show respect," I lied. The words tasted bitter.

"Bullshit." If she had wings, they'd be twitching. "This isn't respect." She tilted her head back and met my gaze with narrowed eyes. "What aren't you telling me?"

"We are investigating Ignarath movements," I deflected, forcing my gaze forward. "Focus."

Her jaw tightened. A muscle jumped beneath the smooth skin of her cheek. "Fine. *For now*." The promise of future confrontation hung heavy, unspoken. "Where to?"

I gestured ahead, upward. The central path carved its way through the city's vertical layers, toward the peaks. "The High Overlook. Ryvik has a scheduled aerial patrol. He'll give us a report."

We climbed in silence that stretched thin as spun glass. The path steepened. The air thinned, carrying the scent of sulfur and distance. Her breathing deepened, audible now, a counterpoint to the thrumming in my own chest. Still, she matched my stride. No complaint. No weakness. Determination was etched in every line of her. She was unshakeable as the mountain itself.

The Overlook. A wide stone tongue thrust from the rock face. It was panoramic as we looked outside of the city and onto the desert that surrounded us. Brutal beauty under the harsh glare of the twin suns. Molten gold light splashed across the crimson deserts below, illuminating the distant, angry shimmer of magma rivers snaking across the blasted land.

Hawk moved past me. To the very edge. Her

steps slowed. The sheer vastness hit her. I watched her profile, etched sharp against the unforgiving light. She was staring out. Something shifted in her expression. It softened. Almost fragile.

"Beautiful," she breathed, the wind snatching the word away. "Terrible beauty."

I came to stand beside her, careful to keep my distance. It was the space she demanded. "Yes."

"From up here ..." Her eyes traced the distant scars of old lava flows, the jagged peaks of the Crystal Mountains where Ignarath territory clawed at the horizon. "I can almost forget the danger." A pause. "Almost."

"Volcaryth is unforgiving," I agreed. "But there is something special out there, for those brave enough to look."

She glanced at me, something unreadable flickering deep in her eyes. "I miss the sky." The admission seemed to surprise even her. A crack in the armor. Vulnerability slipping through. "Before ... on Earth ... flying was everything. Freedom. Perspective. Being grounded here ..." Her voice trailed off, roughened.

"You were a warrior of the skies." It wasn't a question. I'd seen how she watched the Drakarn wheeling high above Scalvaris. There was hunger in her eyes.

A desperation I'd only seen in Drakarn after terrible accidents and shattered wings.

"The best." It was flat certainty. No pride, just fact. "A fighter pilot. Combat-trained. I could make a jet dance on thermals you wouldn't believe." A short, sharp laugh. It was utterly devoid of humor. "Fat lot of good those skills do me here. Just another grounded, useless soldier."

Something tightened deep in me. Pressure. An unnamed ache. "You were born for the sky," I heard myself say, the words emerging unbidden, raw from my throat. "It's in you."

Her head snapped toward me, surprise widening her eyes. For a heartbeat, she just stared. Seeing me? Truly seeing past the scales, the wings, the tail?

"Let me take you," I offered, the words tumbling out before reason could catch them. "Flying."

She froze. Naked longing warred with deep-seated caution across her expressive features. "You mean ...?"

I extended my wings slightly, just enough for the membranes to catch the unseen currents rising from the city far below. The iridescence caught the light. "I am strong enough. To carry you safely."

Her gaze locked onto my wings. She examined the intricate webbing. The powerful musculature beneath. Her breath hitched. A small, sharp sound, audible even over the wind's sigh. There was a spark in the charged air between us.

"Wouldn't that be ..." She hesitated, searching for the word. "Isn't that too ... *personal?*"

"A warrior-carry," I clarified quickly, desperately grasping for the flimsy excuse. "For evacuation. Rescues. It's a standard technique." The lie felt hollow, brittle, even as I spoke it. There was nothing standard about this.

Nothing standard about the fire her nearness ignited.

She should refuse. She should see through the pathetic justification. She should recognize the danger—not just of falling, but of being held so close to me, of trusting her fragile human body to my strength, my straining control.

"Yes," she said instead, the word breathless. Defiance? Trust? Madness? "Take me flying."

My heart slammed against my ribs, a violent drumbeat that surely she must hear, feel. "Now?"

Her smile bloomed then, sudden, fierce, transforming her face. Alive. "No time like the present, Stone Fist."

"Khorlar," I corrected, the rough syllables of my name raw in my throat.

"Khorlar," she echoed, softer this time.

The sound of it settled deep in my bones. Like finding home after centuries adrift.

I moved to the very edge of the platform, letting my wings extend to their full, vast span now, catching wind as it battered them. Turning to face her, I held out my arms.

"You'll need to hold on tightly." My voice sounded strange to my own ears—rougher, deeper than usual. Thicker. "Arms around my neck. I'll secure you with one arm around your waist, but I need the other free for balance."

She approached slowly, her eyes never leaving mine, that fierce determination written in every line of her body. She stepped inside my guard, into my space. She was close enough that her scent enveloped me, a wave threatening to drown me. Making my fangs pulse with white-hot need.

"Like this?" Her arms slid around my neck, warm and tentative against the cool scales.

Not tentative enough. The touch burned. Not nearly enough space between us.

"Higher," I managed, my voice a strained rumble from deep in my chest. "And tighter."

She adjusted her grip, pressing herself against me, her slight weight warm and solid against my chest plates. My arm encircled her waist, claws carefully angled away, retracted, from her fragile human skin, holding her securely against me.

I wrapped my tail around her thigh, and she gasped.

"Only an anchor," I assured her.

Too close. Her heartbeat hammered against my scales, a frantic rhythm echoing my own. Her breath, warm and quick against the sensitive ridge of my throat. I could feel every tense line of her body, the subtle tremor of anticipation—or fear?—running through her.

"Ready?" I asked, the word choked, barely intelligible through the sudden tightness in my throat.

She nodded, her face turned up to mine, those remarkable eyes wide with something caught between terror and raw exhilaration.

I stepped off the edge.

Wings spread wide, catching the updraft. We didn't fall. We *plummeted.*

Just for a terrible second. Her grip tightened convulsively, a small, choked sound torn from her throat—not quite a scream, more a gasp of pure shock. Then my wings bit the air, found purchase, and the plummet became a powerful glide, a surge that carried us away from the mountain face and out over the vast, terrifying expanse of Volcaryth.

Her face buried itself against the hardened scales of my neck ridge, her arms clinging with desperate strength. I could feel her rapid heart-hammer against my ribs, her quickened breath misting against my skin. Beneath the sharp tang of fear rising from her, something else bloomed—pure, unadulterated excitement. Wonder.

"Open your eyes, Hawk," I murmured, my voice a low vibration that hummed between us. "See what I see."

Slowly, tentatively, she lifted her head. I watched her expression transform—fear melting away, replaced by stark awe as she took in the world spread beneath us like a wrathful god's tapestry. The city of Scalvaris fell away behind, a sprawling monument of dark stone and flickering crystal carved into the mountain's bleeding heart. Before us stretched the endless crimson deserts, the distant shimmer of lava flows etching fiery, incandescent veins across the tortured landscape.

"Oh my god," she breathed, the words catching on the wind, ripped away. "It's ... it's incredible."

I banked, riding the thermal currents higher, giving her a broader, more devastating view. She laughed—a sound so unexpected, so pure and unrestrained, that it struck something deep within me, cracking it open. Her body relaxed fractionally against mine, fear forgotten, burned away in the raw rush of flight.

For a precious, stolen moment, nothing else existed. Not the looming Ignarath threat, not the corrosive lie festering between us, not the burning, consuming need that gnawed at me day and night. There was only the wind whistling past, the immense sky arching above, and Hawk secure in my arms, her face alight with a joy so radiant, so fierce, it defied the desolation below.

Mine.

The word echoed through the chambers of my mind, inescapable and absolute. It was a truth branded onto my soul.

All too soon, inevitably, I banked again, beginning our reluctant return arc toward the Overlook. Her grip tightened instantly, a silent, desperate protest against our descent.

"Not yet," she said, the words half-lost, whipped away by the wind. "Please."

I shouldn't. Every second with her pressed against me like this was torture—exquisite, brutal torture. My control was fraying, shredded thin by her scent, her warmth, the terrifying, unconscious trust she'd placed in me. A blade twisting deeper with every beat of my wings.

But I couldn't deny her. Not this. Not when flight had returned something essential to her spirit, something the grounding had stolen.

"Hold on," I rumbled, the sound deep, resonant. I felt her arms tighten around my neck again, her body molding closer still as I caught another powerful thermal and soared higher, carrying us in a wide, sweeping arc that revealed the distant Crystal Mountains, their faceted peaks glittering like cruel diamonds in the harsh sunlight.

Her laugh pealed out again, wilder this time. It was freedom itself given voice. The sound burrowed into me, taking root somewhere deep and vital, somewhere I couldn't reach, couldn't protect.

Eventually, inevitably, gravity and duty pulled us back. I landed with precision honed over the years. But I was frozen. I couldn't let her go. She remained in my arms, her face flushed with exhilaration, her eyes bright, shining with an emotion I couldn't decipher but felt reflected in my own turbulent core. Potent. Dangerous.

Then, slowly, reluctantly, she unwound her arms from my neck. The loss of her warmth was a physical pain, a sudden, hollow ache that gaped open as she stepped back, putting crucial space between us once more.

"Thank you," she said, her voice softer, huskier than I'd ever heard it. Her scent had changed subtly, heightened by adrenaline and something deeper, sweeter, more fundamentally *her*. It was intoxicating.

My tongue felt thick, hypersensitive, burning with the taste of her lingering on the air between us. My vision narrowed, focused laser-sharp on the pulse hammering visibly in the delicate curve of her throat, the slight parting of her lips as she caught her breath.

The moment stretched, taut as a bowstring drawn to its limit. It was vibrating with unspoken tension. I could step forward. One step. I could tell her the truth. I could claim what was already mine in all but name, seal it there under the unforgiving eyes of the twin suns.

Her gaze dropped. Lingered on my mouth. On my fangs, visible now as my lips pulled back fractionally in a silent snarl of need. Something shifted in her expression—awareness flickered, heat kindled deep in her eyes, confusion warring with something else. She swallowed hard, the movement drawing my focus with agonizing precision to the vulnerable line of her throat.

Mine. The word roared through me, a furnace blast drowning all reason, all centuries of hard-won restraint.

Then she stepped back again, decisively this time, breaking the moment. Breaking the connection. Her arms crossed over her chest, an unconscious, immediate barrier. "We should get back," she said, her voice steadier now, though a subtle tremor still vibrated beneath the surface. "You had business with Ryvik, right?"

Duty. The mention was a cold shock, dousing the internal fire. I forced my wings to fold completely, forced my stance to relax, though every muscle fiber screamed with coiled tension, with thwarted instinct.

"He will find us if it's urgent," I managed, the words rough-edged, scraped from my throat. "We should return to the city."

We walked back down the steep path in silence. But it wasn't the same silence as before. This one crackled, thick with unspoken words, with the ghost of flight, with the dangerous heat that had flared between us. Her scent had irrevocably changed, carrying notes of exhilaration and spice and something uniquely, terrifyingly *Hawk* that hadn't been there before the flight. It drove me toward the edge of madness with each shared breath.

As we reached the lower levels, the familiar bustle of the city surrounded us again—too many scents vying for attention, too many clashing sounds grating on over-stimulated nerves. It was overload. I was drowning in sensation, in the crushing weight of restraint, in the lie that felt heavier, more poisonous with each passing moment.

I couldn't do this. Not now. Not with her so close, her altered scent clinging to my scales, the memory of her warmth branded onto my skin, the image of her face alight with joy seared into my mind.

"Return to our quarters," I said abruptly, the command harsher than intended, cutting through the street noise.

She stopped dead, tension rippling through her small frame like a shockwave. "Excuse me?"

"There are matters I must attend to. Alone." I couldn't look at her, couldn't risk her seeing the raw hunger, the fraying control in my eyes. "Return to the quarters. Wait there. I will join you later."

"That wasn't the deal," she countered immediately, anger flaring hot beneath her words, sharp as obsidian shards. "I'm not going back to being locked up while you—"

"Please." The word tore from me, raw, exposed. Utterly unlike me.

Her breath caught, a sharp intake of surprise flashing across her face, silencing her mid-sentence. I had never begged. Never pleaded. Not until now. For this.

Something in my expression, my voice, must have revealed too much. Shown the crack widening in the dam of my control. Because she hesitated, the anger faltering, replaced by a flicker of ... understanding? Caution? Then she gave a slow, reluctant nod.

"Fine," she said quietly, the fight draining out of her, leaving behind a weary tension. "But this conversation isn't over, Khorlar." A promise.

I watched her turn and walk away, each retreating step driving the knife of deception deeper into my own chest. The lie between us had never felt more vast, more damning. But telling her the truth *now* ... after the deception, after the intimacy of flight, after seeing that spark ignite in her eyes ...

I couldn't bear to see the fragile trust, the exhilaration, twist into betrayal. Revulsion. Not yet. Not until I could offer her a choice that wasn't merely the lesser of two evils.

So I turned away, forcing myself in the opposite direction, heading deeper into the city's labyrinthine core. Away from her scent. Away from temptation.

Away from the truth roaring in my blood, rapidly becoming impossible to deny—that I was bound to her, claimed by her as surely as if the Sacred Flame itself had forged the chain between us.

CRACK.

The sound ripped through the cavern. My fist. The dummy shuddered.

Sweat slicked my back; my muscles burned. I spun. I ducked low. Kicked—vicious, satisfying. The post groaned.

Again.

The word was a rasp in my throat. I circled back. My limbs trembled, overworked, but the movements stayed sharp. Precise. I needed this. Needed the ache, the sting blooming across my knuckles. Needed the proof my body could still obey, could still fight.

Not just wait. Not just be ... kept.

Across the hall, Vega and Kira flowed through sparring forms, a blur of controlled violence. Lexa wrestled with a Drakarn guard twice her size, finding leverage. These sessions were small comforts. Brief moments where we were still a unit, not scattered pawns.

Not confined. Not watched.

Not dealing with the heat that flared in Khorlar's eyes. That damned heat.

Another punch. Harder. A grunt tore loose. The leather was my frustration. The stone walls were my cage. Khorlar's constant presence, his suffocating vigilance ... the way my traitorous body hummed when he was near.

This. Was. Better. Pain I understood.

"Hitting like that, you'll break something." It was Selene. I hadn't heard her approach. Her medic's gaze was already cataloging the damage.

"I know what I'm doing." I flexed my stinging fingers. They still worked. Good. The sharp throb grounded me.

An eyebrow lifted. She knew better than to push. Smart. "I'm heading back soon. Vyne's sending guards."

"Babysitters." The word was spat out, bitter. Another punch jarred my arm to the shoulder. Drown it out. Drown *him* out.

Selene's face softened. Was it pity? Understanding? I hated both. "Terra's trying, Hawk. Trying to keep us safe without—"

"Caging us? Treating us like property?" My words were too sharp. Shit. "Sorry. I know she is."

She nodded. She got it. "Vyne says the Ignarath are still holed up in the diplomatic guest quarters. No sign of their 'witnesses' at the Temple."

Lying bastards. They were stalling. Waiting. For what?

I straightened, wiping sweat from my brow. I felt gritty. Real. "Waiting for backup? Or an opportunity?"

"Vyne thinks so too," she murmured, her voice low.

Vega's whistle cut the air. Time was up. Figured. The others gathered their gear, reluctance in every line of their bodies. Back to stony cages.

The timekeeper pulsed—crystal water shifting behind carved stone. Twenty minutes. Twenty minutes until he arrived to escort me.

My escort. My guard. My ... whatever he was.

Twenty minutes of my own.

"I'm cleaning up," I called to Vega, nodding to the water channels flowing in a side alcove. "I'll be fine."

Vega frowned, her warrior instincts screaming. "We should stick together."

"Khorlar's meeting me here anyway."

She hesitated. Then gave a tight nod. "Don't make me come looking."

"Wouldn't dream of it."

I watched them leave. Two young Drakarn flanked them. Faceless guards. The moment they turned the corner—blessed silence. A slow exhale.

Just me.

Cool water sluiced over my face, my arms, shockingly cold against my flushed skin. My reflection stared back—dark skin, damp hair clinging to my temples, eyes too bright, restless. Wild.

A predator pacing its cage. That's what I saw.

I dried off and gathered my things. Ten minutes left. Too long. Too damn long to stand there waiting.

The thought sparked—hot, defiant. I could get back alone. I knew the way. Main corridor. Past the gathering space. Narrow passage. Siege quarters. His quarters. Where he'd put me.

Simple.

And if I ran into him? So what.

I needed this. Needed to walk my own path. Just once. To control something.

It had been days since our flight. Since that ...

whatever that was. Heaven in the skies. Then temptation when we landed. I'd woken up on a moan more than once, imagining what might happen if I invited the hulking granite alien into my bed.

His bed.

Whoever's bed.

It was fucking madness, and I needed to get a damned grip.

I slipped out. My footsteps were ghosts on the stone. Dim light came from the heat crystals. Warm. Secretive. A few Drakarn passed. Their eyes lingered—they saw a human, female, alone—but they moved on. We were novelties, not quite threats anymore. One day maybe they would look at us like we belonged.

I snorted out a laugh. Yeah, right.

I found the main corridor. It was wider there. Ceiling soaring, carved with ancient battles. I stayed near the wall. Moving fast, purposeful. Nothing to see. Just a human.

Halfway there.

The air shifted wrong. A pressure change. The scrape of scale on stone—too quiet, too deliberate. Not the usual rhythm.

My hand twitched for my knife. It should have been there. Wasn't.

I slowed. Every nerve was singing. Scanning the shadows, the deep alcoves lining the passage. Too empty. Too quiet. The mountain was holding its breath.

And then—him.

He slid from a side passage I hadn't seen. Poison-yellow scales. Gleaming sickly in the low light. Not Khorlar's deep gray. He was smaller. Leaner. But still huge.

Ignarath clan-bands were on his arms. Cold dread coiled low in my gut.

This was the wrong place. Far from the diplomatic suites. Terra said they were confined. He definitely wasn't supposed to be there.

"Human." It was a hiss. His tongue flicked out. Tasting the air. Tasting me. Obscene. Predatory. My skin crawled. "Alone. How ... convenient."

My body locked into a combat stance before thought. Low center. Hands loose. Ready. "Exactly where I'm supposed to be." Voice level. Calm. Liar. My eyes scrambled for escape routes. None good.

And this spot was secluded. No one would hear me scream.

A smile. Fangs. Sharper than Khorlar's. Needle-thin. Vicious. "I think not."

He moved. A blur. Faster than anything that big should be. Lunging. Claws reaching for my arm.

I sidestepped—barely. I felt the air stir where my flesh had been. I pivoted. Elbow strike—hard—into the softer scales under his ribs. I aimed to break.

A grunt. Surprise more than pain. It bought me a second. Back up. Assess.

Bad.

Oh, fuck, this was bad.

"It still fights," he hissed. Was there appreciation in the sound? Twisted. It made my stomach clench. "Good. The claiming ... sweeter. I get to show you your place."

He lunged again. Feinted left, grabbed right. Too fast. His claws closed, a scorching steel trap around my upper arm. Pressure just shy of breaking skin. He yanked me off-balance. Toward him.

I fought back.

Everything I had. A kick to the knee that would cripple a human. A strike to the throat just grazed him as he jerked back. Years of training. Instinct.

Not enough.

He was bigger. Stronger. Hungry.

"Let go, shithead!" I snarled. Twisting, trying to break the hold.

Refuse the fear. Don't show it.

"Unaccounted for," he murmured, voice oily, vibrating against my skin. It made me want to retch. "Plaktish will reward this. A gift."

I drove my knee upward. Groin? Something else? I didn't care. I had to hurt him.

He twisted and avoided the worst. His grip loosened fractionally. But I managed to wrench free, my arm burning. I ducked low. Darted past. Back toward the training hall. I needed backup. Now.

His tail whipped out—a blur of scaled muscle. It caught my ankle and sent me sprawling. Stars exploded behind my eyes as my side slammed into unforgiving stone. Air punched from my lungs, leaving me gasping.

Before I could move, he was on me. His clawed hand clamped around my throat. Squeezing. Threatening. Dragging me toward the side passage.

"Struggle," he whispered, breath hot, foul. Against my face. "I enjoy it."

Terror. Fury. A boiling cauldron inside me. I fought like a cornered animal. My elbow smashed into his jaw. Hard. His head snapped back. I felt the bone connect. His grip loosened—*yes!*—and I twisted away.

He recovered too fast. Lunging again, his claws

caught my shirt, and fabric ripped. He hauled me backward.

Kicking, I connected with his knee. I felt savage satisfaction as he let out a grunt of real pain. He didn't let go. His other hand tangled in my hair. Pain flared across my scalp.

"Enough," he snarled, enjoyment gone. Replaced by cold purpose. "You—"

ROAR.

Thunder. Primal. It shook the stone, the air, my bones. Dust rained from the ceiling.

I knew that roar.

Khorlar.

He materialized from the shadows. A nightmare. Vengeance given form. Coiled muscle. Lethal grace. His wings flared—immense—filling the passage. A wall of dark membrane, scaled edges sharp as blades. His eyes—burning gold. Pure, undiluted fury. Blinding.

The Ignarath's grip went slack. Shock. Just an instant. Enough.

I threw myself forward. Broke free and rolled, scrambling to my feet. Fight or run?

Too late. Khorlar moved in a blur. Unholy speed. Claws—wicked death—closed around the Ignarath's throat. He lifted him. Lifted him off the ground. Effortlessly.

"You. Dare?" Khorlar's voice—unrecognizable. A guttural snarl ripped from the mountain's core. "Touch. What. Is. Mine?"

The Ignarath choked. Struggled. His claws scrabbled uselessly at Khorlar's grip. Iron. Unbreakable. "Diplomatic ... immunity ...," he gasped. "Law ..."

"I am the law here." It was a growl vibrating with killing intent. Khorlar slammed him against the wall. Stone cracked. Spiderwebbed. "And you defile sacred ground."

I was frozen. My heart battered my ribs like a trapped bird. Relief. Terror. Adrenaline—a dizzying cocktail.

I should move. Help? I was useless. Transfixed by the violence. The sheer power.

Ignarath eyes bulged. Khorlar's grip was tightening. Millimeter by millimeter. This was an execution. Right here. Right now.

Then—abruptly—release. The Ignarath crumpled. Gasping. His hand clawing at his bruised throat.

"Run," Khorlar commanded. The word was a

low vibration. A deadly promise. "Run to Plaktish. Tell him what awaits those who touch my woman."

The Ignarath scrambled up. Hatred blazing yellow. Spitting fury. "Not over," he hissed, backing away. Vanishing into the shadows he came from. "We will collect. All of them."

Gone.

Silence slammed back in. Khorlar stood rigid. Trembling. Barely contained fury radiating off him in waves. His wings still half-spread. Chest heaving. Rough, wild breaths. He didn't turn. Didn't look at me.

Not for an eternity.

Then he turned. Slowly. The look on his face—rage, yes. But underneath ... something raw. Exposed. Something that cracked my own defenses.

"Sarah." My name. Rough. Unfamiliar on his tongue. Three strides. He closed the distance. His hands came up—huge, clawed—grasped my shoulders. Firm. Careful. Not the Ignarath's violation. This was ... different. Terrifyingly different. "Hurt?"

"It's Hawk," I corrected. Automatic. Voice shaky. Damn it. "Fine."

His nostrils flared. Scenting me? His gaze raked over me. Burning. Possessive. It made my skin flush hot, then cold. One hand moved. To my throat.

Where the other had been. His touch was feather-light. Gentle. Examining.

"Bleeding." It was a low growl. His fingers ghosted a scratch on my arm. I hadn't felt it. "I will hunt him down."

"Nothing," I insisted. My heart was still trying to pound its way out of my chest. "I've had worse in training."

His eyes narrowed. Pupils slitted. His predatory focus zeroed in. "Alone. You should not have been alone. Why leave without an escort? Without me?"

The accusation snapped me back. My spine stiffened. Defenses up. "I don't need a babysitter, Khorlar. I can handle myself." The defense felt weak given the bruises blooming on my throat.

"Clearly," he snarled. He waved his hand toward the empty corridor. The ghost of the threat.

"I was handling it," I shot back. Liar. Fool.

"He would have taken you." His voice dropped. Low. Vibrating. Making me shiver in a way that was completely unrelated to fear. Not entirely. "To Ignarath. Do you know what they do? To females? To you?"

The raw terror in his voice. For me. It gutted me. Cut through the anger, the pride. Left me ... adrift. Relief battling fury battling fear battling ... this.

This thing that sparked between us. This unwanted, undeniable pull.

He was looking at me like I was ... vital. Like losing me would break him.

My lips were dry. I was suddenly aware of how close he was. The heat pouring off him. The sheer size of him. "Sorry," I managed. The word felt foreign. Thick. "I shouldn't have left. I just needed ... space."

His expression shifted. Softened? It was hard to tell with the harsh planes of his face. "From me?"

"From everything," I admitted, honesty tearing loose unexpectedly. "I was feeling trapped. Protected. From—" I cut off. Couldn't say it.

From the fire you start just by looking.

I shook my head. Stepped back. Created distance. My legs wobbled. Ah, there it was. Adrenaline crash. It hit me like a physical blow. I stumbled as reality hit. What just happened. What *almost* happened.

Instantly, he caught me. His arm was like a steel band around my waist. Steadying. Solid. "Sarah—"

"Hawk," I whispered. No heat left. Just exhaustion.

"Hawk," he amended. His voice was softer now.

Gentler than I'd ever heard. Than I thought possible. "You're safe now. I have you."

Something snapped. Some final defense crumbled. I didn't think. Couldn't. I leaned into him. My forehead pressed against the hard planes of his chest. Scaled, but warm. So warm.

He went utterly still. Tense. Like I might shatter.

Then, slowly, carefully, his arms came around me. Enfolded me. Strong. Secure. His wings followed—a living shield of dark leather and scale. Blocking out the passage, the fear, the world. Just him.

I should have pulled away. Rebuilt the walls. Insisted on distance.

Should.

Couldn't. My heart racing—not just fear now. My body trembling—not just adrenaline. He held me fast.

Safe. Terribly, confusingly safe.

His heat soaked into me. Chased away the bone-deep chill. His scent—hot stone, wild spice, him—filled my lungs. Familiar now.

Comforting? God, help me.

"Sorry," he murmured again. The vibration against my cheek. A physical thing. "I should have been here. Protected you."

I shook my head. Mutely. My fingers curled into the rough scales of his chest. Clinging. Seeking an anchor in the storm.

"What do you need?" he asked. Simple. Loaded. Heavy with everything unspoken.

I didn't think. Couldn't process. Just ... answered. The raw truth bubbling up from the chaos.

"Take me flying," I whispered. My voice thin. Barely there. "Please."

I felt his breath catch. His arms tightened. Fractionally. He pulled back just enough to see my face. His golden eyes—molten, intense—searched mine. Saw ... what?

"Anything," he said. The word absolute. A vow carved into the sudden stillness. Burning itself onto my soul.

WE DIDN'T SPEAK. Not one word.

Not when those impossible arms swept me up—a cage of stone and heat. Not when his wings like scarred night unfurled, swallowing the weak corridor light. Not when we shot upward through a vertical shaft, a sickening, dizzying spiral that *should* have ripped a scream from my lungs.

Instead? Nothing. Just ... a weird, wild uncoiling deep inside.

My fingers dug into him—hard muscle, cool rough scales beneath me. It was instinct. I was grounding myself against the impossible. His scent hit me again—that volcanic stone and something else, something sharp, primal, male—and my lungs hitched on a shaky inhale. His arms weren't just strong; they were ... possessive.

Careful, yes, but with a crushing undercurrent. Like I was something fragile. Something he owned.

That thought *should* have triggered pure rage. It should have.

But it didn't. Why?

The shaft opened. Sky. Endless, bleeding red sky. Twin suns hemorrhaging light across the horizon, painting this broken world in raw, wounded color. Then the heat hit—a physical blow, a violent updraft flinging us higher. My stomach vanished. A choked gasp tore free, involuntary. His grip tightened instantly. Possessive. Protective. Both.

We soared.

Below was Volcaryth, sprawling, impossible. Hidden ledges, dark openings. And beyond—nothing. Crimson waste stretching forever. Lava rivers like molten veins. The distant, deadly shimmer of the Crystal Mountains. Ignarath territory. Poison.

Wind ripped at me—my hair, my torn clothes, my sanity. It tried to slash away the terror still clinging from that corridor. From what *almost* happened.

He climbed higher, his wings beating—a powerful, steady rhythm vibrating through his body, into mine. Solid muscle worked beneath my desperate grip. Living steel. Raw power, ruthlessly contained.

But I could feel it—the tension coiled tighter than before. Darker. Sharper.

This wasn't the controlled flight from the other day. This was ... fury unleashed. A raw, jagged edge to his movements. His breathing—harsh, audible even over the wind—betrayed the inferno still banked beneath the scales.

Rage. At the Ignarath warrior. At the situation. At me? Or something deeper, something tied to that burning look in his eyes?

He banked—sharp, sudden. My breath hitched as instinct took over again. I clutched tighter, pressing myself against the unyielding wall of his chest. His heart hammered under my palm—too fast, too hard. A war drum echoing the frantic beat in my own ribs.

"I would have killed him," he bit out, voice a low growl nearly lost to the wind. Each word was obsidian sharp. "Should have."

The first words. They shattered the charged silence.

I swallowed past the sudden dryness in my throat. "Not worth the diplomatic incident." My voice sounded thin, reedy.

Something rumbled through him, deep in his

chest, sinking straight into my bones. "Worth *everything.*"

That conviction—raw, absolute, scraped from somewhere deep and terrible—sent a shiver down my spine that had nothing to do with the altitude. Or maybe it did.

His eyes found mine. Gold fire. Burning away pretense. Burning away *me.* "He touched you."

It was not a question. It was a verdict. A wound ripped open.

"He didn't get far," I managed. I forced steadiness into my voice. I was a liar.

His nostrils flared. Was he scenting me? My lingering fear? The echo of the other male's proximity? Or something else—something stirred by his own words? "Far enough."

Silence again. Thick with it. His wings worked, catching currents rising from the cooling rock below. Effortless grace masked the storm inside. The tension didn't vanish—not in him, not between us. It just ... shifted. Twisted into something less like rage, more like ... anticipation. A wire pulled taut. Waiting.

Time dissolved. I lost track. Lost *myself* in the steady beat of his wings, the solid pressure of his arms, the impossible, terrifying freedom of the open sky. This. This was what I'd craved since crashing here. This vastness. This escape.

With him. *Because* of him.

Damn it. My brain circled back, trapped in the contradiction. Hating the cage, needing the bars? Needing the *keeper*? The way he watched me ... the way I was starting to watch him back.

No. Stop.

The light shifted. The suns sank lower, shadows stretching like grasping fingers across the scarred land. Reluctantly—I felt it in the shift of his muscles—he began the descent. We spiraled back toward the mountain. Toward the city. Toward the cage.

"Thank you," I whispered, the wind stealing the sound. But his grip tightened fractionally. He heard. Acknowledged.

We didn't return to the shaft. We landed instead on a narrow stone platform—a balcony carved into the rock face, tucked away, facing the cooler, shadowed side of the mountain. Private. Isolated.

His wings folded with a soft leathery sigh as his feet touched down. But he didn't release me. Not yet. He held me there, suspended, my face level with his. Close. Too close. Close enough to see the faint pulse in his throat, the rigid line of his jaw. Close enough to feel the heat radiating off him. Close enough to drown in those burning gold eyes.

Slowly. Deliberately. He lowered me. My boots scraped stone. His hands lingered at my waist—heavy, hot. Was he steadying me? Or just ... unwilling to break contact?

Both.

"Better?" His voice was low. Rougher than the wind.

A simple word. An impossible question.

I nodded. I couldn't trust my voice. The flight had scoured the panic away, yes. But it replaced it with ... this. This trembling awareness. This awful, dangerous curiosity.

We stood there. Inches apart. His hands still branded my waist. His wings, not fully retracted, created a partial enclosure. Trapped us in a bubble of scale and heat and fading light. Just us.

"You frightened me." Each syllable sounded dragged from his throat. Like a confession ripped free. Or an accusation.

My spine stiffened. "I wasn't trying to—"

"I'm not angry." He cut me off, sharp. "Frightened." He repeated the word like it tasted bitter. Like the admission cost him something vital. "When I saw him ... touch you—" He broke off. Jaw grinding. A muscle jumped near his temple. "When I couldn't find you. When I thought—"

Something cracked. Raw. Undone. Right there in his voice. Made my own chest physically ache in response.

"I'm okay," I said. The words felt stupid. Useless. Untrue.

"No." A shudder rippled through him. Visible. His wings trembled. "Not okay. None of this ... is okay."

Before I could process that, could even think, he turned. Released me abruptly. Created distance. A chasm opening between us. Protecting me? Or himself?

"We should return," he said, voice clipped. Controlled again. But the current underneath ... it was volatile. Barely contained. Dangerous.

I should have nodded. Said nothing. Let the distance stand. Maintained the lie—protection, duty, alliance. Nothing more.

Instead, I stepped forward. Closed the gap. "Khorlar."

His head snapped around. Eyes blazing—pure gold fire. Pupils contracted to sharp vertical slits. His focus absolute. Terrifying.

"What aren't you telling me?" My voice was

steadier than I felt. A reckless challenge. "About the Ignarath. About me. About ... this." I gestured vaguely at the charged air between us, thick with unspoken things.

He sucked in a harsh breath. His chest rose, fell. Was he steadying himself? Or preparing? "You don't understand." Rough. Bitten off. Like the words physically hurt him. "You can't understand."

"Try me." A dare. A stupid, stupid dare.

A mistake.

He moved. That impossible speed again—stone to liquid fire in the space between heartbeats. His hands clamped onto my shoulders. Not rough. Not exactly. But ... inevitable. Decisive. Nowhere to run.

"It's not protection," he admitted, the words torn raw from somewhere deep. Primal. "Not *just* protection."

I wanted to flinch back. My survival instincts screamed at me to *move*. But my feet were bolted to the stone. My body—traitor—held fast. Heart trying to hammer its way out of my ribs.

"What then?" A whisper. Barely audible.

His hands slid. Slow torture. One cupped the side of my face, thumb brushing my cheekbone— rough heat. The other back to my waist, drawing me closer. Inch by agonizing inch. Not forcing. Asking.

Demanding. Claws carefully, pointedly retracted. Just warm, hard palm against the thin fabric of my shirt. Then bare skin.

"This," he growled. Low in his throat.

And his mouth crashed down on mine.

Fire. Nothing but fire. Consuming. Absolute.

Shock first—the alienness of it. Lips firmer than human, impossibly hot. A scaled texture at the edges. His taste—wild, sharp, elemental heat, utterly male— exploding through my senses. My hands flew up to his chest—to push him away? To cling on? Didn't know. Didn't matter.

Then instinct surged. Older than reason. Deeper than fear.

I kissed him back.

A sound ripped from his chest—a growl, a groan. Hunger. Victory. Relief. His hand tightened at my waist, hauling me flush against his furnace heat. Body to body. An inferno. His other hand tangled in my short hair, rough scales scraping my scalp, angling my head. Deepening the kiss. Demanding. Taking.

And I gave. God help me, I gave it all.

My fingers clenched, digging into the hard scales of his chest. Trying to find purchase in the hurricane. I found the frantic thunder of his heartbeat beneath. Matching mine. Beat for desperate beat.

His tongue—hot, surprisingly soft but with a textured roughness—traced the seam of my lips. Asking. A question buried in the certainty. I parted for him. Let him in.

The taste of him—scorched spice, primal heat, pure male—seared through me like lightning. Obliterated thought. Caution. Sanity. Left only raw, aching *need*. The slick glide of his tongue tangled with mine. The careful, terrifying edge of fang brushed my lower lip—sensation blurring pain and pleasure. Control. Even now, that terrifying control.

A sound tore from someone's throat—desperate, broken, needy. Oh god. Me. It was me. Shame flared —hot, brief—then vanished, swallowed by the firestorm coiling low in my belly, burning through every vein.

His hand slid under my shirt hem. Scalding palm flat against the bare skin of my back. Tracing my spine. Gentle. Deliberate. Each brush of his fingers a brand. A claim. Making me his.

I arched into it. Into him. Pressed closer. Needed closer. That sound again—mine? His? I didn't know. Didn't care.

"Sarah," he groaned against my mouth. My name.

My *real* name—a prayer and a curse torn from his throat.

Ice water shock. Reality crashing back.

I wrenched away. Gasping. Stumbling back on trembling legs. I put space between us. Heart hammering so violently my vision pulsed at the edges. Air searing my lungs.

What— What just—?

What had I *done*?

His eyes—wild, unfocused gold fire—locked onto mine. Pupils blown wide, then snapping back to sharp slits as control warred with instinct. The hunger there—naked, raw, unfiltered—sent another wave of sickening heat washing through me.

"I—" he started. Stopped. Jaw working. Utterly lost. His chest heaved. Wings still half-unfurled, trembling with reaction.

I touched my lips. I felt the burn. Tasted him still. Fire and spice. Him.

"I'm sorry," he finally managed, the words rough, dragged from somewhere deep and painful. "I should not have—"

"No," I cut him off, surprised I had a voice. Surprised it was almost steady. "It was—"

What? What *was* it? A mistake? Stress?

Captivity fever? The inevitable explosion of *this*—this impossible, terrifying connection?

None felt right. None captured the earthquake that had just leveled every wall I'd ever built.

"It just ... was," I finished lamely.

He understood. The unspoken hung heavy between us. His eyes—molten gold, burning with something far more complex than just desire—held mine for another long, shattering moment. Then he looked away. Forced a deep, shuddering breath. Forced his wings to fold tight against his back. Stone warrior assembling himself piece by painful piece.

"We should return," he said again. Voice tight. Strained. But underneath—that barely restrained wildness still thrummed.

I nodded. Once. Mutely. Couldn't speak. Couldn't trust myself.

He approached. Slowly this time. Carefully. Asking permission with his eyes, his stance. Maintaining a sliver of distance. I stepped into his space. Into the heat radiating off him. Let him gather me up again, tuck me against his chest.

It was different now. Everything different. Charged. Every point of contact a spark, a live wire humming with dangerous energy. But his touch was

... formal. Impersonal. Almost. Despite the inferno I could still see banked deep in his eyes.

The flight back was silent. A heavy, suffocating silence thick with everything unsaid, everything suddenly, irrevocably changed.

We slipped back through the shaft. Back into the stone throat of Scalvaris. Back toward the cage. Our quarters. The shared space that suddenly felt impossibly small. Suffocating.

I turned away. Faced the wall. Needed air. Needed space. Needed to not feel the ghost of his mouth on mine.

"Hawk," he said. Quietly. That low, rough growl that sent an entirely unwelcome shiver tracing fire down my spine.

I risked a glance over my shoulder. His face was closed off again. Impassive stone. But his eyes—always the eyes—betrayed him. Still burning. Still hungry. Still remembering.

"I must attend to Council matters," he said, the words stiff. Formal. "I will return later. You'll be safe here."

Translation: *I* need to get away from *you*. Now.

"Fine," I managed. I hated the breathless edge clinging to my voice. "Go."

He hesitated. A flicker in his eyes—was there

more to say? More to *do*? Then a sharp, decisive nod. And he was gone. The door clicked shut, leaving me alone.

Alone with the echo of his taste searing my lips, the phantom heat of his hands on my skin, and the terrifying, burning certainty that whatever line had existed between us—duty, protection, captor, captive —had just been incinerated.

And I had no idea what was going to grow out of the ashes.

8

KHORLAR

PRIMAL INSTINCT IGNITED, a fire searing itself onto my thoughts: *Hunt.*

The word was a blood-beat thrumming in my ears, drowning out reason. The lingering taste of her—that intoxicating sweetness still sharp on my tongue—fueled the rage that had smoldered since I'd seen that Ignarath filth put his claws on her.

My female. *My* claim.

Remaining there, breathing the air thick with her scent and my own unraveling control, was impossible. The stone walls of our quarters pressed in, confining, suffocating. Her expression, shifting from the heat of desire to confusion, then back to that guarded wariness I knew too well, was a blade twisting in my gut. I turned and ran, claws gouging stone as I descended into the deeper levels.

The killing-need throbbed behind my fangs. The Ignarath was still there. Still breathing Scalvaris air. Still polluting a world where he'd dared to touch what was *mine*.

It was unacceptable.

Diplomatic immunity. Temple law. Council politics. They were dust motes in the face of the storm roaring through my blood, the ancient imperative that demanded retribution. That demanded his life.

Deeper now, where the air hung thick and still, I caught it—the faint, oily musk of Ignarath, laced with the sharp tang of fear-sweat. A grim satisfaction curled in my gut. Good. Let him fear. Tonight, I would teach him its true meaning.

My pace slowed as I reached the lower levels. These were less traveled. Darker. Heat crystals pulsed sporadically, spaced far apart, casting long, skeletal shadows across the rough-hewn passages. It was a perfect hunting ground. He thought distance meant safety down there among the forgotten ways.

Fool.

"Khorlar."

I spun, a snarl ripping from my throat before the disciplined part of my mind registered the speaker. It was Zarvash. His bronze scales absorbed the low light, gleaming dully. He watched me, his gaze typically calculating, yet sharper, more perceptive than usual.

"Not now, Zarvash," I growled, the sound rough even to my own ears. I turned away. The hunt pulsed, a living thing inside me. I had no time for Council subtleties. "I am owed blood."

"You mean the Ignarath delegate?" His voice—cool, measured—was like stone scraping against my frayed control.

I froze. Turned back slowly, the heat rising behind my eyes. "How did you know?"

"I have eyes," he replied simply. His stillness was a counterpoint to my simmering violence. "And I have the ability to recognize a warrior consumed by a blood hunt." A slight, deliberate tilt of his head. "He touched your human." He said it so surely. He wasn't guessing. His spies must have given him a report.

My human.

The words, spoken aloud by another, sent a fresh wave of burning possessiveness surging through me. The claim—certain, absolute—was undeniable now. Not after that kiss. Not after feeling her response, tasting a hunger that mirrored my own fierce need.

"He tried to take her." The words rumbled, ripped from somewhere deep in my lungs. "He would have dragged her back to Plaktish."

Zarvash's eyes narrowed fractionally, the only outward sign of his assessment. "That's crossing lines, even for Ignarath arrogance." A pause, weighted with calculation. "You intend to kill him."

It wasn't a question. It was a statement of inevitable fact.

"Yes." There was no hesitation. No doubt.

To my surprise, Zarvash gave a single, decisive nod. "Good."

I blinked, taken aback. The Strategist was never so direct, so ... approving of naked aggression. He was always weighing consequences, maneuvering through political currents. "You believe me?"

A flicker of teeth in the gloom—not quite a smile, something sharper. "I believe what my senses tell me. My sources tell me that Plaktish flew here with five Ignarath, though only four were presented to the Council. This one has been conspicuously absent from official functions." His copper-streaked wings shifted, a subtle rustle in the quiet. "Convenient."

Understanding dawned, a cold, sharp clarity cutting through the red haze of rage. "A shadow operative. Unsanctioned."

"Precisely." Zarvash's tail gave a slight flick, a gesture of grim satisfaction. "Which means ..."

"His life is forfeit under Scalvaris law." The realization tasted sweeter than honey-mead. There was no diplomatic shield. No Council interference. Just justice, raw and immediate.

It meant just blood.

Zarvash's head tilted. "Need assistance?"

The offer was unexpected. Zarvash commanded strategy, not close-quarters combat. But the look in his eyes held a flicker of something deeper—an understanding that transcended mere territorial disputes.

"No." This kill had to be mine. Alone. The insult was personal; the retribution would be also. "But ... I appreciate the information."

He inclined his head, accepting my decision. Then, unexpectedly: "This way." He turned, melting with surprising silence down a narrow side passage I hadn't noticed, barely more than a fissure in the rock. "He favors the abandoned storage caverns. Thinks himself unwatched."

I followed, the anticipation of the hunt tightening every muscle, honing every sense to brutal clarity. The air grew heavier, thick with dust and the musty scent of long disuse. Every drip of moisture, every skittering pebble echoed in the oppressive silence.

The passage widened abruptly into a cavern, vast

and shadowed. It was once a storage chamber, now empty save for drifts of dust and the ghosts of forgotten supplies. A perfect hiding place. A perfect killing ground.

And there—stronger now—was the distinctive musk. It was fresh. He was close.

Zarvash faded back toward the entrance, a silent ally positioning himself to cut off escape. He was not interfering. Just ... ensuring. I gave him a curt nod of acknowledgment, then advanced deeper into the cavern's heart, my claws silent on the dusty stone floor.

There was a scrape of scale against rock. It was too loud. Too deliberate.

I whirled, wings flaring instinctively, a shadow expanding in the gloom, just as a blade whipped through the air where my throat had been a heartbeat before. The Ignarath—sickly yellow eyes wide with a potent cocktail of hate and fear—lunged from behind a crumbling pillar, desperation lending his movements a wild, unpredictable fury.

"You should have fled Scalvaris when you had the chance," I rumbled, satisfaction a dark curl deep within me. This was better than an ambush. Face to face. Warrior to scum.

"You broke the compact!" he snarled, circling warily, his blade held low. "The Temple—"

"Temple law offers no sanctuary to shadow-claws operating outside of Scalvaris hospitality." I matched his movements, step for predatory step, letting him feel the weight of my presence, the certainty of his doom. "You are unregistered. Unacknowledged."

Raw fear flashed across his face, momentarily eclipsing the hate. Good. Let him understand. No protection waited for him there. Only death.

"The female isn't yours," he spat, desperation making him reckless, stupid. "Plaktish has plans for all those sky-fallen."

Red. The world dissolved into a haze of pure, killing red. Thought ceased; only the imperative remained.

I lunged.

Not the measured attack of a disciplined warrior. This was older. More primal. Sheer, unmitigated rage given form.

He was fast—credit where it was due. His blade sliced upward, catching a stray beam of light from a distant heat crystal. But I was beyond caution, beyond pain, beyond anything but the need to silence him, to end the threat he represented.

My claws found his weapon arm first, shearing through scale and muscle, grating against bone. He screamed—a high, thin sound that was abruptly satisfying. His blade scored a burning line across my shoulder—a flare of pain quickly consumed by the greater fire within me.

It was unimportant. Nothing mattered but ending him.

He tried to twist away, seeking escape, but I surged forward, wings flaring wide to block his retreat, herding him back against the rough, unforgiving stone of the cavern wall. His eyes darted frantically, twin points of terror seeking an exit that wasn't there. Finding only me.

"What she is," I snarled, advancing steadily, claws digging into the stone, "is utterly beyond your squalid comprehension."

The fear-scent emanating from him was thick now, almost cloying. It was prey fear. Perfect.

"She's nothing!" he spat, a final, futile burst of defiance. "Just human meat! Just—"

My hand clamped around his throat, fingers digging deep, cutting off the filth spilling from his mouth. I lifted him, his own weight aiding the pressure. His claws scrabbled uselessly against the thick scales of my forearm, drawing blood I barely felt. His eyes bulged, the yellow irises swimming in white. Terror now. Raw. Absolute.

"She," I growled, the word scratched from somewhere ancient and possessive within my soul, "is *mine*." The claim resonated, a binding truth spoken into the shadowed space. "And you *touched* her."

Truth. Sentence. Execution.

One sharp, brutal twist. The sickening crack echoed, swallowed by the vastness of the cavern. It was finality. Silence.

I let the body drop, a limp weight thudding onto the dusty floor. Satisfaction warred with the lingering rage in my blood. It wasn't enough. He should have suffered longer, paid more dearly for daring to lay his filthy claws upon her. For threatening her. For the *plans* he mentioned ...

No. I couldn't allow my thoughts to linger there. That path led toward a madness I couldn't afford.

"Efficient," came Zarvash's cool voice from the entrance. It was calm. Approving. "If somewhat ... intense."

I turned, my chest still heaving, the metallic tang of blood—his and mine—sharp in the air. It cooled quickly on my scales in the cavern's depths. "He deserved far worse."

"No argument," Zarvash replied, moving forward to examine the corpse with detached, clinical interest. "I will arrange for this ... disposal. Quietly." A pause, then those assessing copper eyes fixed on me again. "Your human must be truly ... remarkable."

Something in his tone snagged my attention. It was not mockery. Not judgment. A flicker of something akin to ... understanding? Or perhaps merely strategic curiosity. Strange, considering Zarvash's feeling on human mates only a few months ago.

"She is," I stated simply. Denying it now, after this, would be pointless. Futile.

That flicker of teeth again, the not-quite smile. "Interesting times lie ahead, Khorlar." He gestured with his snout toward the gash across my shoulder, where blood still welled sluggishly. "You should have that tended to."

I grunted. The wound was shallow. Nothing. Already clotting against the cool air. "I need to return to her."

His expression shifted minutely, a subtle acknowledgment. "Of course." A knowing look that, coming from anyone else, would have ignited my fury anew. From Zarvash ... it felt merely perceptive. "The Ignarath will not attempt this again. Not directly. Not after this message has been ... received."

"They had better not." The growl rumbled, low and menacing.

"No." His gaze flicked briefly to the corpse. "I believe the point has been made quite clearly."

I left him there to manage the aftermath, trusting his discretion, his strategic mind. Trusting him to ensure this act of necessary justice wouldn't create inconvenient political ripples for Darrokar or the Council.

The killing rage had subsided, leaving behind something just as powerful, but colder, sharper. A bone-deep certainty. A fierce, unwavering protectiveness that resonated beyond duty, beyond honor, beyond even the primal claiming-fever of the bond.

She was *mine*. And I would eradicate anyone, anything, that dared threaten her.

My steps quickened as I ascended, heading back toward our quarters, toward *her*. The drying blood—his and mine—caked on my scales would need cleansing before I faced her. She couldn't see me like this. Not yet. The warrior unleashed was not something she was ready for.

But soon ... soon we would have to confront what simmered between us. What had been undeniable from that first shared glance across a field of wreckage, that first intoxicating brush of her scent. Soon, she would need to understand the truth.

She wasn't merely under my protection.

She was under my skin. In my blood.

9

HAWK

I SAT on the edge of the sleeping platform, my fingers tracing the cool, smooth silk beneath me. I stared at nothing. My lips still felt ... bruised. Not painful, exactly. Just thoroughly kissed. The memory —Khorlar's heat, the scrape of fang against my lip— played on a loop behind my eyes. Heat bloomed low in my belly just thinking about it.

The door scraped open. A slice of corridor light appeared, then shadow filled the frame. Khorlar.

His shoulders were rigid. The way he held his weight was wrong. Even silhouetted, I knew.

"You're hurt," I said, the words sharp. I was on my feet before the thought finished forming.

His nostrils flared, a subtle shift in the dim light as he stepped fully inside, and the door hissed closed. The air shifted with him, carrying a scent sharper than his usual smoke and scorched metal—ozone, maybe? And underneath, faint but undeniable, copper. Blood.

"It is insignificant," he said, his voice rougher than usual, like stones grinding together.

Liar. My gaze snagged on the dark, wet patch dulling the scales of his left forearm. It was a gash. And I noticed the almost imperceptible favoring of his right leg.

"The Ignarath?" My throat tightened.

His eyes, molten gold in the gloom, found mine. Something dangerous flared there—old, predatory, deeply satisfied. "He poses no further threat."

The finality of it hung in the air. Cold. Efficient. A shiver traced my spine, but it wasn't fear. More like ... resonance. A dark chord struck deep inside. He'd dealt with a danger. To me. *Because* of me.

"Sit." I pointed to the platform, adopting a tone I usually reserved for malfunctioning equipment. "Now."

A muscle ticked in his jaw. "The wounds are shallow."

"I wasn't asking." It was old habit. Assume command when things go sideways.

Surprise flickered across his harsh features, quickly masked. Then, almost amusement? He gave a stiff nod and moved to the platform, lowering himself with a control that didn't quite hide the strain. His wings rustled, settling like folded shadows against his back.

I grabbed water and cloths. My movements felt jerky, too fast. Back in the main room, Khorlar watched me, his stillness a counterpoint to my buzzing nerves. I knelt before him, setting the basin down with a soft click. I was closer than strictly necessary. The air between us felt thick, charged.

"Arm." I held out my hand, palm up.

He hesitated for a heartbeat, then extended the limb. The gash wasn't ragged but clean, deep enough to part scales, revealing the darker, vulnerable flesh beneath. Dried blood flaked away as I touched the edge. I dipped a cloth, the cool water darkening the fabric.

Starting at the edge, I cleaned gently. His scales were cool and smooth under my fingers, almost like stone, transitioning abruptly to the raw edge of the wound. He didn't flinch, but I felt the tension radiating from him, a low hum beneath the surface.

My thumb brushed against an intact scale. Hard, unyielding.

A low rumble shook his chest, dismissive. "Desperation lends false strength." His eyes burned into me, tracking my every small movement. "His words sealed his fate."

I looked up, the cloth poised in my hand. "His words?"

"Regarding Plaktish. Regarding ... intentions for you." The gold in his eyes turned golden, lethal. "Unacceptable intentions."

Unacceptable. My stomach clenched. Not with fear. It was something else. Possessive heat. I dipped the cloth again, needing the focus. "You killed him. For saying things."

"For intending them," he corrected, his voice flat. "For daring to voice them in my presence. For touching you. Trying to hurt you. I would rend him apart again."

There was no hesitation. Just fact. The heat in my gut intensified, spreading outward. I shifted my attention, spotting another tear in his tunic, dark blood staining the fabric near his ribs.

"Shirt off," I ordered, my voice huskier than intended.

He went utterly still. For a long second, the air crackled. Then, with a fluid ripple of muscle, he pulled the tunic over his head, tossing it aside.

Oh. *God.*

Gray scales flowed over muscle, defined and

dangerous. Scars, pale lines against the dark crimson undertones, mapped old battles. And the rings. Twin hoops of dark metal pierced his nipples, catching the faint light. Primitive. Provocative. My fingers twitched.

Focus. I pressed the damp cloth to the shallow cut on his ribs. His muscles jumped, abs clenching hard under my touch. His breathing hitched, growing rougher. Not from pain. Definitely not from pain. His tail twitched once against the floor. A restless whip-crack sound in the quiet.

"Leg?" I asked, my eyes fixed on the scrape I was cleaning.

"A bruise," he grumbled. "It requires nothing."

I finished, setting the cloth aside. The silence stretched, thick with unspoken things. His scent filled my lungs—ozone, hot metal, and something intensely male, musky underneath. I started to pull back. "All done. Don't get it—"

He moved like lightning striking. One hand tangled in my hair, tilting my head back. His mouth crashed down on mine.

It was not like before. There was no caution here. This was raw. Starvation unleashed. A claiming.

My gasp was swallowed whole. My hands flew to

his shoulders, gripping hard scales, anchoring myself as his tongue swept inside. Longer than human. Hotter. Textured ridges scraped against my own tongue, sending shocks straight down my spine. Smoke, metal, the coppery tang of his blood, and pure, undiluted Khorlar. Intoxicating.

"*Vrakasha,*" he groaned, the alien word a vibration against my lips.

I didn't know it. Didn't care. *More.*

My fingers dug in, nails scraping against the unyielding surface. A deep growl answered me, rumbling from his chest into mine. He surged to his feet, lifting me effortlessly. Air rushed past as he pinned me against the wall. Cool stone pressed against my back, his scorching heat branding my front. I moaned into his mouth.

"*Yes,*" he snarled, less a word, more a guttural agreement. His hands found my thighs, strong fingers digging in as he hitched my legs around his waist. His mouth left mine to plunder the side of my neck. Fangs grazed my pulse. Not breaking skin. Promising. Threatening. My head fell back, offering more.

The hard ridge of his cock pressed against my belly, insistent through the layers of our clothes. His hips rolled, a slow, deliberate friction that lit a firestorm between my legs. I arched against him, desperate for the contact.

"Clothes," I gasped, fumbling at the fastenings of his trousers. "Too many."

A sharp, guttural sound of assent came from him. His mouth returned to mine, devouring, as his claws made short work of the tough fabric. His cock sprang free, thick, dark crimson, glistening. Dark scales covered the base, fading into flushed, impossibly swollen flesh. That strange, mobile lip at the head pulsed. My breath caught.

My own clothes disappeared in a tangle of limbs and frantic need. Torn fabric joined his tunic on the floor. We were naked. I was gloriously, terrifyingly naked against him. He pulled back, his tail unwinding from its resting place to snake up my inner thigh, the tip leaving a trail of gooseflesh.

"Look at you," he breathed, his voice rough, almost reverent. Golden eyes devoured me. "Open for me."

Shame warred with a defiant surge of heat. I didn't cover myself. My gaze dropped, tracing the powerful lines of his chest, the hard planes of his abdomen, down to the thick, alien shaft straining toward me. Pre-cum beaded at the tip, catching the light like a dark jewel.

"Bed," he commanded, his voice dropping into a register that resonated in my bones.

My legs trembled as I slid down the wall. I took two steps toward the platform, but his tail whipped around my waist, hauling me back against his chest. Hard muscle, cool scales, radiating heat. I gasped.

"Every inch," he murmured, hot breath ghosting against my ear. "I will taste *everywhere*. Mark you until your scent screams *mine*."

Was it offensive? It should be. But it wasn't. Heat pooled, heavy and demanding, between my thighs.

His tail released my waist, the tip tracing a teasing path down my spine as I crawled onto the platform. Cool silks against burning skin. It was a moment's relief. Then he was there, looming over me. His wings flared, plunging us into deeper shadow, a world shrunk to just the two of us.

The tip of his tail returned, dancing between my legs. Teasing strokes against slick folds, circling my entrance but never pushing inside. Never giving me the friction I craved. I writhed, hips lifting off the sheets.

"Please," the word ripped out of me, raw and unfamiliar.

"Please *what, vrakasha*?" That word again. Dark

honey and threat. "Tell me." His voice was a low growl near my ear.

"You. Inside. *Now*." I reached down, trying to guide him.

His hand clamped around my wrist, pinning it gently above my head. "Patience." A predator's rumble. His mouth descended, closing over my breast. That tongue—long, rough, unbelievably hot—rasped across my nipple. I cried out, arching hard.

"So sensitive," he purred against my skin, pure masculine satisfaction. "Trembling for me." His tail resumed its wicked game, sliding through the wetness, stretching me just enough to torment. "So wet."

It was truth. My body screamed its betrayal, its need. His mouth moved lower, leaving a trail of fire over my ribs, my stomach. I knew where he was going. I couldn't stop him. Didn't want to.

The first touch of his tongue to my core—I shattered. It was deeper than human. Rougher. The ridges created an almost unbearable friction. His hands gripped my thighs, parting me further. He consumed me. Relentless focus.

"Taste ...," he growled into me, the vibrations shaking my bones, "like fire. Like mine."

His lips closed around my clit. Fangs, a hair's

breadth away. Delicious danger. He suckled, tongue working magic, and the world dissolved. Orgasm slammed into me, stealing breath, stealing thought. My back bowed off the silks, a scream tearing from my throat, his name echoing in the small space. My fingers clawed at his shoulders, seeking purchase in a world gone white-hot.

He didn't stop. He kept lapping, sucking, working me through the aftershocks until I was limp, trembling, skin exquisitely oversensitive. Only then did he lift his head, golden eyes blazing with fierce, possessive pride.

"Beautiful," he rasped, crawling up my body. He kissed me, deep and slow. I tasted myself on him. The intimacy stole my breath all over again.

I felt the thick, blunt pressure near my entrance. Not his cock. His tail. More insistent this time. "Let me," he murmured, voice ragged against my throat. "Prepare you. Don't want to hurt ..."

Before I could form words, he pushed inside. It was slow. Inexorable. The tapered tip stretched me, scales providing a rippling, alien friction. Not pain. Just ... fullness. Strange perfection.

"Easy," he coaxed, his voice strained. "Take it."

His tail moved within me, a slow, deliberate invasion. Stretching, curling, learning my depths.

Finding places I didn't know existed. Each internal ripple sent sparks behind my eyes. His mouth worked my throat, my collarbone, leaving damp heat and the faint sting of fang marks. He was branding me.

I was dissolving under the dual assault, writhing, gasping his name, pleading without words. He withdrew his tail. A moment of shocking emptiness. Then it was replaced. Hot, blunt, impossibly thick. The head of his cock nudged against my opening.

"Look at me." One large hand cupped my jaw, forcing my gaze to meet his. Molten gold burned into me. "Watch."

Eyes locked, he pushed inside. Slowly. That ridged, pulsing lip at the crown nudged against hyper-sensitive flesh. Stretching. Burning. Filling me completely. He was bigger. So much bigger than human. The texture—scales grading into velvet heat —was utterly alien, utterly consuming.

"Tight," he groaned, his control shredding. Fangs grazed his lower lip. "Gods ... *perfect.*"

He sank deeper. Inch by agonizingly slow inch. His wings trembled. Restraint was costing him. When the scaled base of him finally met my slick flesh, he paused. Let me adjust. Let the overwhelming fullness settle. Stuffed. Claimed. Completed.

Then. He. Moved.

The first thrust was deep. Hitting bottom. A choked cry tore from me. Instinct took over. My legs wrapped around his waist, heels digging into the base of his spine, just above where the tail joined his body.

"Harder," I sobbed, nails scoring crimson paths down the black scales of his back.

A roar ripped from him, primal and terrifying. He slammed into me. Faster. Deeper. That strange structure at the head of his cock pulsed, stroked, rubbed with every withdrawal, driving me insane. Finding nerves I didn't know I had.

We moved together. Flesh against scale. Silk twisting beneath us. We created a frantic rhythm. Sweat slicked our bodies. His scent—ozone, metal, musk—filled the air, thick and heavy.

"*Mine,*" he snarled, biting the juncture of my neck and shoulder. Not gently. Marking me. The word vibrated through my bones. "Say it, *vrakasha.*"

"Yours!" The word ripped free, torn from a place deeper than thought. Primal. Honest. In that moment, nothing else existed. His. Mine.

His rhythm broke. Thrusts became erratic,

desperate. He was almost losing control. The scaled base ground against my clit, friction building unbearably. His tail lashed around my thigh, squeezing hard, mirroring the frantic rhythm of his hips.

"Come," he commanded, his voice thick, guttural. "With me. *Feel* you."

That final, deep thrust. The grinding pressure. The command. It shattered me. My inner muscles clenched around him, milking him. His answering roar shook the room, vibrating through the floor, through me. I felt his release flood me, hot, thick, branding me from the inside out. His pulses echoed my own climax.

Silence crashed down. Khorlar collapsed, his weight pinning me, his forehead pressed to mine. His wings draped over us like a fallen curtain. I felt his tremors, the harsh rasp of his breathing mingling with my own ragged gasps. He pulsed weakly inside me still. Echoes of the storm.

Eventually, agonizingly slowly, he shifted, rolling onto his side but pulling me with him. His arm banded my waist, his tail a heavy, possessive coil around my thigh. Claiming, even in exhaustion.

No words. What could be said? Inevitable disaster? Necessary collision? Both? My mind spun, trying to calculate consequences, risks. Warnings screamed silently.

But I didn't pull away. I couldn't. I curled closer, my cheek finding the solid, steady beat of his heart beneath the scales. His arm tightened. Cool scales against fevered skin.

A mistake? Probably. Definitely. But as darkness pulled me under, wrapped in his heat and scent, I couldn't regret a single second.

10

KHORLAR

THE DIM CHILL in the depths of Scalvaris seeped through stone, a pale imitation of true darkness, but instinct recognized the shift. My eyes snapped open. I was alert and ready.

And saw *her*.

Hawk. My mate.

The truth slammed through me, undeniable as bedrock, resonant as a war drum. She was curled against my side, her dark skin highlighted by the muted glow filtering from the heat crystals in the walls. One slender arm lay heavy across my chest, her fingers instinctively gripping the edge of a scale even in sleep. Her heat radiated against me—not the scorching fury of Volcaryth, but something softer, deeper, soaking past my scales to the cold stone core of me.

Mine.

Something low rumbled in my chest, a sound of pure ownership I barely contained. Evidence marked her—the faint bruising where my fangs had grazed her fragile skin, the shadow beneath where my claws had held her hips. It was proof. Possession. The air hung thick with the scent of our joining, her human musk interwoven with my own harsher tang. It was intoxicating.

She stirred, the rhythm of her breath snagging. Her muscles tensed beneath my arm. Consciousness returned like a snapped bowstring. Her eyes opened —dark pools reflecting the low light—and locked onto mine.

Vulnerability flashed there, raw and exposed. Gone in a heartbeat. Her shield slammed back into place, that wariness I recognized, honed sharp by survival. Yet beneath it, embers still glowed hot. The contradiction clawed at my control.

"Mine," I grated, the word rough-edged, torn from my throat. My hand moved, unbidden, tracing the line of her shoulder. Scales met skin. She shivered, a tremor that sparked fire low in my gut. "My mate."

Her body went rigid, a wire pulled taut. She

didn't recoil. Not yet. The claim hung between us, heavy as unmined ore.

"A heavy word," she finally breathed, her voice thick with sleep but losing none of its edge. Always that edge.

I leaned closer, filling my lungs with her scent. Ours. "I know what matters." My voice dropped lower, scraping like stone on stone. "Enough."

Our faces hovered scant inches apart. Her breath feathered against my jaw. Her eyes searched mine—for lies? Weakness? She found neither. Only the unyielding certainty of my claim.

A shuddering exhale escaped her lips. Not surrender. Never surrender. But ... something shifted. Her fingertips, tentative, brushed the half-healed ridge of the wound on my shoulder. It was where I bled defending *her*.

Ignition.

I captured her mouth, crushing any response. A choked gasp escaped against my lips, then she melted, resistance shattering like heat-shocked stone. Her arms snaked around my neck, fingers digging into the sensitive juncture where scale met flesh. It was a pressure point. She knew.

A possessive growl tore from me. I rolled her beneath me, pinning her with my weight, wings flaring instinctively, casting us in deeper shadow. She was mine to shelter. Mine to command. She arched upward, body remembering, yielding where her mind still fought. My claws, retracting just enough not to break skin, gathered her wrists. One hand pinned them above her head. The other traced fire down her side, mapping the curve of her hip.

"Tell me to stop," I challenged, the command guttural.

Defiance flared in her eyes, warring with the flush rising on her skin. "Don't ..." she gasped, her legs parting, inviting the invasion. "command me." Then, softer, desperate. "Just ... don't stop."

Her fight, even in surrender—it drove me toward a precipice. I released her wrists, seizing her hips instead, angling her. Ready. Slick heat met me. Her body, honest and urgent. I drove into her. One smooth, deep thrust. Her eyes flew wide, her back bowing sharply off the sleeping platform.

"Khorlar." My name, a broken sound. A plea. A brand.

I set a brutal pace. Each thrust was a staking of territory. Each withdrawal was a promise. Her nails raked my back, scoring paths near the vulnerable base of my wings. Pleasure sharpened, bordering pain. Our bodies moved, a frantic rhythm, two forces colliding, forged for this clash.

"What *is* this?" she demanded between ragged breaths, her eyes finding mine, refusing to break contact even as tremors shook her. Always the questions. Always pushing. "Mate? What does it mean? To you?"

My rhythm stuttered. A fraction of a second. The question hit harder than her nails. The answer thundered through me, stark and absolute.

"Everything," I snarled, driving deeper, harder. Watching the war on her face—fear, need, defiance. "You are ... everything. Strength. Weakness. Honor."

Her eyes widened. Fear flickered. Real fear. "And to your people? Scalvaris?"

I caught her face between my hands, rough, forcing her gaze. Our bodies slammed together. Opposing tides. "Mine. To protect. To defend." Words failed me. How to explain the path ahead without shattering her fragile courage? "There are ... challenges. Those who will not accept."

Her jaw locked beneath my grip. "I don't need protecting."

A harsh laugh escaped me. "And yet, you have it. Want it or not."

Something fractured in her gaze. Anger. Need.

A reluctant yielding. Her inner muscles clenched, milking a groan from my depths. "Not a cage," she warned, her voice strained, even as her body pulled me closer, deeper. "Not yours. Not anyone's."

"Never," I ground out, my pace quickening, the edge rushing toward me. "A fortress."

She shook her head. Denial warring with imminent release. I felt it begin—the tightening, the sharp inhale. I thrust harder, pulling the sound from her, her cry echoing my name like a shattered vow.

My own release roared through me. Unstoppable. Consuming. I collapsed, bracing my weight, burying my face in the curve of her neck.

Her scent. Mine.

Silence pulsed afterward. Fragile. Tense. Her breathing slowed beneath me. Her hands, hesitant now, rested on my back, tracing scale patterns. Thinking. Always thinking.

Knock. Knock. Sharp. Intrusive.

"Councilor." A young guard's voice, tight with urgency, muffled by the stone door. "Darrokar requires you. The Ignarath demand audience."

A silent snarl peeled my lips back. Plaktish. Testing. Or perhaps Zarvash wasn't as discreet as he said.

Beneath me, Hawk stiffened. An instantaneous

shift. Soft yielding replaced by coiled alertness. The warrior surfaced. It called to the beast in me.

"Inform Darrokar I'll attend shortly," I called back, irritation roughening my voice.

"Councilor." Retreating footsteps echoed, swallowed by the stone.

She slid from beneath me. Moving with fluid grace, utterly unashamed of her nakedness. It was armor as much as vulnerability. The breach I'd made in her defenses was sealing itself, stone by silent stone.

"Trouble?" Her voice was carefully neutral. She was gathering torn cloth.

I rose, my eyes narrowed, tracking her every move. Precise. Efficient. It was a fighter's economy of motion. She would never be docile. Pride warred with a sharp stab of frustration.

I regretted nothing. Flat. Final. "He touched what is mine."

Annoyance? Uncertainty? It flickered across her face like heat lightning. "I'm not a *thing*, Khorlar."

"No." Three strides closed the distance. I pulled her against me, ignoring the brief stiffening. Her strength against mine. "Far more dangerous."

Before she could form a retort, I took her mouth again. Hard. A statement. Pulling back, I saw the conflict still raging in her wide eyes. Desire warring with defiance.

"I'll return when this is settled," I promised against her lips. "No one takes you from me. Understand?"

She didn't answer. Her gaze held mine, a silent challenge. "Plaktish," she said instead, her voice low. "He plots. Be careful."

Fierce pride swelled my chest. Even now, torn as she was, her mind worked, assessed threats. For *me*. Confirmation hammered home. My match. Whether she admitted it or not.

"Stay here," I commanded, turning toward the door. "The guards are posted."

Her expression tightened. "Cages, Khorlar."

"Necessity," I countered, pausing at the threshold. "They showed their hand. They *will* try again."

A muscle jumped in her jaw. She gave a sharp nod. Acknowledgment. Not agreement. It would suffice. For now.

I stepped into the corridor. The door hissed shut. My claws curled, digging into my palms. Her scent clung to me, a distraction, a purpose. Discipline. I would need it all. A suspicious Council. A rival seeking blood. A human mate.

And her. The one being who could unravel the control I'd spent a lifetime forging.

I strode toward the Council chambers, the stone cold beneath my feet. Let them come. Let Plaktish scheme. Let the Council whisper. One truth burned through the noise, echoing with each beat of my heart.

Human. Mate. Mine.

I would burn Volcaryth down before I let her go.

I COULDN'T STAY STILL.

My body still hummed. The ghost of his touch was a brand, searing hot across my skin. A deep, radiating ache pulsed between my thighs, but I had to put it out of my mind.

The sheets beneath my restless hands still held his scent. Hot stone, the sharp tang of ozone after a lightning strike, something wilder, more primal. It was him.

He was mine.

The word ricocheted through my skull, his voice —rough-edged, absolute. It was not a request. A goddamn statement of fact carved into the air.

Then came the other word.

Mate.

My breath hitched. Terror, cold and sharp, pierced through the lingering heat. Partner? Lover? These were human concepts. Breakable. Temporary. But mate? That felt heavy. Permanent. Like chains forged in the planet's fire, binding me in ways that went bone-deep, soul-deep.

My fingers grazed the sensitive skin of my neck. Just below the jawline. This was where his fangs had pressed. They didn't break the skin—controlled, even then—but left a faint, damning pressure mark. Evidence. I'd seen the look Selene gave Vyne. Terra and Darrokar. Orla and Rath. That impossible mix—exasperation, fierce loyalty, and something else. Something elemental I couldn't name but felt crackling between them.

And now ... it was me? Just like that?

I had to move. I dressed quickly, slamming my feet into my boots as if I had somewhere to go, as if I hadn't promised Khorlar—my mate!—that I would stay put.

Three steps, then a turn, sharp. Two steps, a halt before the sleeping platform where—no. I shouldn't think about that. Five steps. Water basin. Cold water splashed, stinging my face and neck. It was useless. It couldn't touch the furnace roaring beneath my ribs.

I needed answers. Not from Khorlar. Every time I tried, his damn mouth ended up on mine, his heat overwhelming the questions, my body a traitor to caution. I needed clarity. Distance. Perspective.

Selene.

She was a soldier. A medic. Pragmatic. She'd understand this battlefield confusion. And bonded to Vyne ... she'd navigated this impossible territory. Found her footing. Maybe she could show me the map.

With the decision made, a spark of purpose cut through the haze. I moved to the door and hesitated. Khorlar's warning—his low growl about safety—hung thick in the air. But I wasn't prey to be caged, not even by him. Not even for my own good.

Besides, I wasn't going far.

The corridor pulsed with the low glow of heat crystals. Shadows stretched long and distorted. Guards. Drakarn warriors stood like stone sentinels at points where none had been before. This was Khorlar's doing. My jaw was tight as I pulled my hood lower, kept my head down. I wasn't sneaking, exactly. Just ... avoiding notice. The faint bruising on my neck suddenly felt like a spotlight. No one tried to stop me.

I moved through the lower training quarters and past the medical caverns. The route snaked through quieter sections of Scalvaris, away from the main thoroughfares, away from the few other human faces who might see the flush I couldn't scrub away, the slight tremor in my hands.

Selene's alcove in the medical caverns was small, carved raw from the rock. Shelves lined with bizarrely colored pastes and tightly wound bandages. It was clean. Efficient.

But it was empty.

Shit.

There was no Selene.

Vega, however, was only a bit farther down the corridor. The last person I needed to see right now.

She paced the small space like a caged sand-cat, sharp, contained energy vibrating off her. Her head snapped up, eyes narrowed as I entered.

"Hawk." Relief warred with immediate suspicion. "Where the hell have you been? I came to your quarters to talk to you, and the lizards wouldn't let me pass."

I froze, suddenly hyper-aware of how I must look —clothes rumpled despite my attempts to straighten them, hair probably a mess, the tension still thrumming through me like a plucked wire. "I'm here now," I managed. Vague. Useless. "Looking for Selene."

"She's with Vyne, as usual," Vega dismissed, waving a hand impatiently. "Council crap. Speaking of—" She closed the distance between us. Her voice dropped to a conspiratorial hiss despite the emptiness. "I've been thinking ..."

My stomach plummeted at that look. It was fierce. Burning. The Vega-look that meant caution was already out the airlock. The same look I'd seen while she was scaling a cliff during training, sprained wrist be damned.

"Vega—"

"I overheard some of them talking," she barreled on, cutting me off, eyes glittering. "The Ignarath warriors, the ones with the delegation. They were talking about humans. Not us, Hawk. Others. Survivors."

The word hit like a physical blow. Survivors. The hope that fueled us. The reason we endured. But now ... hearing it ... a strange, hollow dread coiled in my gut. More humans. What would that mean for ... this? For everything?

"I swear I heard one of them say Larissa," Vega pressed, leaning closer, her breath hot with urgency.

"Specifically. That's Kira's sister, Hawk. We have to find out more."

"And they just said all of this conveniently by you?"

She rolled her eyes. "I was on training duty while some of their delegation was working out in the training yard. They stared at me, and I pretended not to understand them when they started spouting off some gross shit. They basically ignored me after that."

I swallowed, the metallic tang of adrenaline flooding my mouth. Forced focus. "And your plan is ... what? A suicide stroll into Ignarath territory based on gossip?"

Her face hardened, jaw set. "I'm not asking permission."

"Clearly," I shot back, the word sharper than intended. Raw nerves frayed by sleeplessness and ... everything else. "You never do."

She actually recoiled. Hurt flashed, quicksilver, then vanished behind anger. "What's that supposed to mean?"

"It means you're about to run off half-cocked based on zero actionable intel," I countered, crossing my arms, needing the barrier. "Again."

"At least I'm doing something!" she snapped.

"While you've been ... what, exactly? Holed up in your gilded cage with your giant lizard bodyguard?"

The barb struck true, a sickening lurch in my stomach. I was focused on Khorlar. On this ... thing between us. Had I forgotten? Pushed the search aside? Guilt twisted, sharp and cold.

"I've been trying to navigate this mess," I defended, the words tasting like ash. "Like the rest of us."

"The last time I 'ran off,' it was to save our people, or did you forget? This is exactly the same."

"It is not, and you know it. Last time you knew exactly where they were and had no reason to think the Drakarn would help. That was months ago; things are different now." My voice was getting louder. I needed to get control of this situation.

Vega's eyes narrowed. Her head tilted, studying me with a sudden, laser focus that made my skin crawl. "What's that?" Her gaze fixed on my neck where the hood had slipped.

My hand flew up. Too fast. A dead giveaway. I yanked the fabric higher, heart hammering against my ribs. But the damage was done. Understanding dawned on her face. Then disbelief. Shock.

"Oh my god," she breathed, barely audible. "You ... and him? Seriously?"

Heat flooded my face, burning up my neck. Shame? Defiance? The emotions churned, inseparable. "It's complicated."

A harsh bark of laughter escaped her. Bitter. "It's fucking stupid, Hawk. That's what it is. Terra, Selene, Orla—fine. Whatever alien voodoo got them. But you? I thought you had better sense."

Anger flared, hot and immediate. A shield. "What's that supposed to mean?"

"It means you're compromised!" she shot back, stepping into my space, voice laced with contempt. "You're sleeping with the enemy while our people could be out there freezing or starving or worse! While we're all trapped in this goddamn mountain!"

"They're not the enemy!" The words sprang out, automatic. Protective. When did that happen? "If they were, we'd be dead. Or worse."

Vega's face twisted. "Listen to yourself! They got you defending them now? What's next? Trading your flight suit for scales?"

I bristled, sucking in a sharp breath. "That's not fair. I want what's best for all of us. I'm still me." Am I? The question echoed, insidious. Or am I being pulled apart?

"Are you?" she challenged, voice dangerously soft now. "Because the Hawk I knew would be halfway to

Ignarath territory already. First boots on the ground. Not ..." She waved a hand vaguely at me, at the tension, the mark I tried to hide. "Whatever this is."

The accusation landed like a fist. Uncomfortably true. Had I lost my edge? Had this ... bond ... this heat with Khorlar ... blinded me? Distracted me from the mission? From them?

"Look," I tried, forcing calm I didn't feel into my voice, "rushing in is suicide. The Ignarath aren't like the Drakarn here in Scalvaris."

"And there it is," Vega pounced, eyes flashing triumphantly. "Terra might be moonstruck over her dragon, but at least she still fights for us! You're just ... hiding."

Terra. Our leader. Still sharp, still focused, even with Darrokar at her side. Had I failed where she hadn't? The comparison stung, sharp and deep.

"I'm not hiding," I insisted, but the words felt thin, brittle.

"No?" Vega stepped back, arms crossed. Pity flickered in her eyes, and that was worse than the anger. "Then help me. Unless ... unless your scale-daddy is more important than finding our people now."

The crude insult scraped raw nerves. "That's low, Vega."

"Is it?" She shook her head, the fire back in her eyes. "Nine women here. There were thousands of people on our ship. Where are the rest, Hawk? Don't you even care anymore?"

The question punched the air from my lungs. Of course I cared. I had to. They were my people. My responsibility. I took an oath to keep them safe. But tangled in this alien heat, this primal pull towards Khorlar ... was that oath still unbroken? Untainted?

"We need a real plan," I said finally. The admission felt like defeat. Like waving a white flag. "To think this through. This is all ... fast."

Vega's expression softened, just a fraction. Disappointment dulled the anger. "We don't have time, Hawk. If they're in Ignarath hands ..."

She didn't need to finish. I remembered the cold hunger in that scout's eyes. The pure hatred. If our people were there ...

"I'll talk to Khorlar," I offered, the words tasting bitter. It was a compromise that felt like betrayal. "Get real intel. Not rumors. If it checks out—"

"You'll what?" Scorn dripped from her voice. "Ask your alien boyfriend for permission to save our people?"

Steel finally entered my voice. Enough. "I'll do

what needs to be done," I bit out. "But I won't lead a rescue mission into a massacre based on a hunch."

She stared at me, a long, assessing moment. Betrayal hardened her gaze again. "You know what, Hawk? I think you have changed. And not for the better." She brushed past me, pausing at the alcove entrance, turning back just enough to meet my eyes. "Just remember who you are. They're not like us. No matter how much Terra or Selene or you want to pretend. They'll never be human."

She left. The silence she left behind was heavy, crushing. Her words echoed in the sudden emptiness.

Not like us.

I stood there, rooted to the spot, the weight of everything pressing down. What had I become? Who was I becoming?

And the question that clawed its way up from the deepest part of me, the one that truly terrified me: was I losing myself?

Mate.

The word pulsed with the heat still radiating from my core.

What did it mean? For me? For my duty? For the women I came here with?

No answers. Just the bone-deep certainty that

the ground had shifted beneath my feet. Something fundamental had fractured inside me, in my world.

There was no going back to the soldier I was before Khorlar. Before this.

The real question, the one that made my breath catch in my throat ...

Did I want to?

THE AIR in the Blade Council chamber was heavy with the metallic tang of old power and fresh tension. It felt less like a council room and more like a cage where predators circled, waiting for the first sign of weakness.

I stalked in, each scale pulled tight against my frame, my control a physical effort, an iron discipline clamped down hard. Every instinct I possessed screamed danger. This wasn't procedure. This was a battlefield disguised by tradition.

The circular chamber was packed, the air vibrating with suppressed hostility. Darrokar stood near the heart of it, a towering presence at the curved stone table. His obsidian scales seemed to drink the light. I could feel the pressure radiating from him.

Around him, the others took their positions. Some faces were stone, unreadable masks hiding gods-knew-what agendas. Others shifted, eyes flicking, calculating—the stink of politics clinging to them.

Rath caught my eye. A grim nod passed between us, a shared current of understanding. He could feel it too. Vyne sat beside him. Across from them, Nyx's gray-and-white marked scales stood out. He was the Shield. Pragmatic. Solid.

His support, if given, would carry weight.

But it was the figure opposite Darrokar that sent a shard of ice scraping down my spine.

Karyseth.

Her silver-streaked scales caught the light like honed blades, throwing back fractured reflections. Her robes, heavy with the symbols of the Forge Temple, whispered against the stone with every calculated shift of her weight. She was power. Cold. Predatory. Behind her, her acolytes stood unnervingly still, yellow robes stark against the dark stone, their eyes burning with a fervor that made my teeth ache.

This wasn't a meeting. It was an ambush dressed in ritual.

"Stone Fist honors us," Karyseth's voice sliced through the tense silence, ancient as the deep rock beneath us, cold as a starless night. Her gaze, sharp and merciless, raked over me, lingering—deliberately—on the still-raw score across my shoulder where the Ignarath bastard's blade had marked me. "Fresh from dealing out justice, it seems."

Every head turned. The weight of their collective stare was a physical pressure. I met it head-on, moving to my place at the table without faltering. Let them look. Let them see the price paid for touching what was mine.

"Our esteemed Council member has been ... occupied," she continued, the curve of her lips showing just a hint of fang. "While one of our guests now lies cooling."

"An uninvited guest," Zarvash cut in smoothly, leaning forward from his seat. His bronze scales caught the light, his voice deceptively mild. "Who trespassed where he had no right."

Karyseth's eyes narrowed to slits. "Blood spilled on Scalvaris soil demands accounting by the Temple. The Temple does not play favorites."

A low growl rumbled deep. "The accounting is simple," I bit out, the words rough. "He tried to take what is mine. He paid the price."

A ripple went through the chamber. Whispers hissed like steam escaping rock fissures. Good. Let the claim echo. Let it become undeniable fact carved into the very stone around us.

"And that," Karyseth said, turning her sharp gaze back to the full Council, her voice rising slightly, "brings us to the poison in our midst." She gestured dismissively, though not towards me. "These humans. Outsiders. They bring only chaos. Their very presence invites Ignarath aggression."

"The humans did nothing to summon Plaktish," Darrokar's authority slammed down, silencing the chamber. A blade forged in command. "The Temple knows this."

"Do not presume to tell me what the Temple knows," Karyseth shot back, her tail lashing the stone once, a sharp crack in the heavy air. "Strange beings from the sky. Possessing knowledge we lack. Bonding with our strongest." Her eyes swept the room, landing briefly, pointedly, on Darrokar, Rath, Vyne, then me. "Altering the balance. We can end this threat without more bloodshed by simply surrendering them."

"Surrender?" Rath snarled, leaning forward, his scales flushing a darker, furious red. The word was an obscenity there. "You mean sacrifice."

"I mean the survival of Scalvaris." Karyseth's

reply was ice against his fire. "One city against its rival. These humans are not our people."

The chamber fractured. Voices clashed, raw and angry. Krazith always bowed to the oldest, harshest traditions. Morvar, whose lands bordered the Ignarath, let fear oil his words. Brezath, ever the opportunist, smelled power in the Temple's stance. Their agreement was loud, insistent.

Others held back, watching, waiting. The calculation in their eyes sickened me. This wasn't about right or wrong for them. It was about advantage.

But the line held. Darrokar was immovable. Vyne's loyalty to his own human mate, Selene, was absolute. Nyx's warrior honor demanded protection once offered. Zarvash, the Strategist, saw the trap in appeasement, even if he was normally an adherent of the temple. Rath's usual recklessness was tempered into fierce, unexpected conviction.

And me. I was rooted to the spot. Unyielding. A wall of stone and fury.

The noise swelled, a cacophony threatening to shatter the fragile control. Darrokar raised a hand, but the momentum was with the dissenters, fueled by Karyseth's burning fire.

I stepped forward again, into the charged space before the table. Fangs bared. The clamor faltered, died down. Expectation hung heavy, thick as volcanic dust.

"No human," I declared, pitching my voice low but letting it resonate with the bedrock certainty I felt in my bones, "will be traded. Not one. The warrior code forbids bargaining lives like chattel."

"You speak of code?" Karyseth challenged, turning fully to face me, her presence a suffocating wave of ancient power. "While shattering tradition? Your human was targeted because you claimed her outside Temple sanction!"

The accusation struck sparks against my pride. "My claim needed no blessing," I growled, the sound ripped from my chest. "It was made by right of blood. Bone. Instinct." My wings shifted, restless, scraping faintly against my back plates.

"Animal instinct," she hissed, dismissing centuries of warrior truth. "Undermining the careful order."

"The order was broken when Ignarath sent a shadow-operative to steal her," I shot back, planting my feet wider. "That wasn't politics. It was an act of war."

"Stone Fist is right," Zarvash added, rising to stand near me, a surprising but welcome solidarity. "The attempted abduction proves the Ignarath are not acting in good faith. They want something specific from these humans."

"The Strategist speaks like an apostate!" Karyseth snapped, eyes flashing. "Placing outsiders above your own kind?"

A harsh laugh scraped my throat. "Safety? Appeasement buys only illusion, Priestess. Never safety."

"Enough!" Darrokar's command wasn't just loud, it was a physical force that slammed into the room. His wings flared, catching the light, a controlled display of the inferno beneath his scales. Every eye locked onto him. "The Temple demands action. The Council requires deliberation. We cannot act until we possess facts."

"We demand a vote!" one of Karyseth's zealots cried out, stepping forward rashly. "The Temple—"

"The Temple advises," Darrokar cut him off, his voice dropping to a lethal softness, eyes narrowing. "The Council decides. And I determine when that decision is made." His wings flared wider, undeniably dominant. "We adjourn. Review strategic implications. All of them. Before any vote."

Karyseth's face tightened, her silver scales seeming to darken. Suppressed fury radiated from her like heat off scorched rock. "The Sacred Flame burns hot, Darrokar. Some threats demand a response."

"And they will receive it," he countered, implacable. "Once we understand why. Why Plaktish is so desperate. Why that specific human was targeted." His gaze flickered to me. A silent acknowledgment that shook me deeper than the open conflict. "There is more at play here."

Strategic brilliance. Buying time. Time to think, gather strength, shore up defenses. My respect for Darrokar solidified into something harder, sharper.

"Word arrived as I entered," Vyne spoke into the sudden quiet, his deep voice resonating. "Another Ignarath envoy approaches. Formal. Escorted."

The air thickened again. A formal envoy. Escorted. This wasn't a probe. It was pressure. A demand backed by implicit threat.

"Then we prepare," Darrokar concluded, drawing himself up. The Warrior Lord incarnate. "Assess the defenses. Identify weaknesses. This Council reconvenes when I call it." His gaze swept the chamber, a final command. "Dismissed."

Karyseth and her acolytes swept out first, their departure leaving a chilly wake. The other Council members fragmented, hushed, urgent conversations breaking out. Lines were being drawn in the stone, allegiances hardening like cooling lava.

"You gather powerful enemies, Stone Fist," Zarvash murmured, pausing beside me, his voice low, meant only for me. "And powerful allies."

I gave a curt nod, my throat tight. "So has she." The name felt raw, scraped from somewhere vital inside me. Hawk. My vrakasha.

"Indeed." His gaze was shrewd, penetrating. "Keep her close. Whatever Plaktish truly seeks ... I suspect your mate is pivotal."

My claws flexed, scraping against the polished stone. A low growl threatened again. "They will not touch her."

"Of that," Zarvash said, a flicker of something almost like a smile touching his lips, "I have no doubt. But blades alone won't win this fight. Stay sharp."

He moved off, leaving me standing there, the echoes of the chamber settling around me like chains. The political maneuvering, the veiled threats, the shifting alliances—it set my teeth on edge. It wasn't clean. Not like battle.

But at the heart of the storm, unwavering, was her. Hawk. My mate. The impossible human who had torn through the stone and scale I'd built around myself.

I turned, stalking from the chamber, feeling eyes track my exit. The tension of the meeting clung like suffocating ash, but beneath it, a different heat burned—fierce, absolute.

Let them come. Temple zealots. Ignarath shadows. Scheming Council members.

They would not take her.

SWEAT DIDN'T JUST SLICK my skin; it plastered my shirt to my back, stinging where the rough training tunic chafed. Every muscle screamed—a familiar, persistent burn. I pivoted hard, the worn floor gritty under my boots, ducking the whistle of a practice staff aimed for my skull.

The kid—Trazek—let out a frustrated hiss, his dark scales rippling. He was young. Eager. Predictable.

I exploited the opening, sweeping low. His legs tangled, momentum stolen. He hit the stone with a surprised whump, air exploding from his lungs. Dust puffed around him.

"Balance," I grunted, not offering a hand yet. I let him feel the impact. "Or height means nothing."

A low chorus of clicks echoed from the shadows

where other warriors watched—the Drakarn version of approval, or maybe just interest in the novelty. These sessions, snatched between whatever passed for shifts here, were less a distraction, more a necessary violence. A way to burn off the corrosive tension coiling in my gut since Vega's accusation. Her disappointment was a physical weight, a phantom hand squeezing my ribs.

But charging into Ignarath wasn't bravery. It was suicide. And I wasn't done living yet.

Trazek scrambled up, ignoring my eventually extended hand. Good. Pride was useful. His eyes glittered with renewed fire. "Again," he demanded, stance resetting, wings flaring slightly.

I circled, letting my gaze dissect his form. It had been weeks of this—watching, fighting, learning. The subtle shift of weight betrayed a lunge. The whisper-faint rustle of wing membranes telegraphed a sideways dodge. The involuntary twitch at the base of the tail revealed his commitment. These were Drakarn tells. Different, but readable.

"Control your tail," I said flatly, nodding toward the appendage that kept flicking nervously behind him. "It broadcasts every damned thought."

His brow ridges furrowed. The struggle was

plain—instinct warring with instruction. "How?" he asked, the question raw curiosity, not challenge.

"Lower center of gravity." I dropped into a fighting crouch, demonstrating. "Core. Leverage. We break differently."

A voice, rough as unpolished stone, scraped from the edge of the pit. "Physics remain constant, human. Only the weak fail to master them."

My head snapped up. It was Elder Vraxxin. Copper scales dulled with age, streaked like old blood. Temple markings etched deep into his shoulder plate—Karyseth's dogmatic mouthpiece. The contempt wasn't even veiled; it radiated off him like a foul heat.

Before the necessary, calculated retort formed on my tongue, Trazek straightened, lifting his chin. He showed a surprising spark of defiance. "Her methods work, Elder. Three victories. She adapts."

Vraxxin's nostrils flared. A dry, dismissive hiss escaped him. "Skills forged on a world without fire-breath or scaled hides. Games." He turned, addressing the watchers, his voice rising, deliberately pitched to carry. "While you indulge this ... curiosity ... the Council splinters. Stone Fist defies wisdom, defies tradition!" His gaze sliced toward me, sharp and accusing. "All to shield these outsiders."

My blood turned to ice water in my veins. Stone Fist. Khorlar.

"The Temple demands censure!" Vraxxin's voice cracked like a whip. His fangs flashed. "Plaktish's warnings cannot be ignored! Stone Fist courts open war—for a human female!"

The warriors shifted, a low rasp of scales on stone. Unease rippled through them. This was not just chatter. It was poison. Carefully dripped into waiting ears. Politics played out with claws barely sheathed.

The words hit me like a physical blow, stealing my breath, cracking something deep inside. The fear I'd pushed down, the gut-level certainty I'd refused to name—confirmed. Khorlar wasn't just risking his standing. He was laying his honor, his command, maybe the fate of his people, on the line. For ... this. For whatever raw, dangerous thing pulsed between us.

A quieter voice, female, came from the back. Bronze scales caught the heat-crystal light. "They fight with honor, Elder. They seek no quarrel."

Vraxxin's tail slammed the ground. Crack! The sound echoed, sharp as breaking bone. "Honor? Wisdom? When Ignarath hordes sharpen their claws on our borders? When the sacred flames themselves show ill omen?" He jabbed a clawed finger toward me. "This is the folly of sentiment! You are too soft."

The bronze warrior stiffened, wings quivering with fury held rigidly in check. Hierarchy. It was brutal and absolute.

Enough. The air was suddenly thick, unbreathable, charged with accusation and the crushing weight of Khorlar's sacrifice. The stone walls felt like they were shrinking, pressing in. I backed away, movements tight, controlled. I dropped the practice staff onto the rack. The clatter sounded too loud in the sudden quiet.

"I need air," I clipped out, forcing the words past the tightness in my throat. I addressed no one in particular.

No one tried to stop me. I walked, measured steps, refusing to run, toward the arched exit. Dignity was armor, even when shattered underneath. Inside? It was a vortex.

The corridors were a maze carved from the mountain's heart. I climbed, seeking height, escape, autopilot steering me toward the eastern overlook. I just needed out. Away from the judgment, the politics, the impossible weight of him.

The air was still a furnace, but it was fresher there. Below, the broken, savage landscape of

Volcaryth sprawled under twin setting suns bleeding violent reds and golds across the sky. A brutal beauty. Raw. Untamed.

Like him.

My palms pressed against the rough-hewn stone railing. Breathe in. Hold. Breathe out. Force the panic down. Fill lungs with air that didn't taste of guilt and a desire that felt dangerously close to treason against my own survival.

A faint rush behind me, the whisper of powerful wings displacing air. Every nerve ending screamed awareness before my brain caught up. Primal recognition. My spine went rigid. There was no need to turn. I knew that sound. Knew that presence.

Khorlar.

I kept my eyes locked on the bleeding horizon, forcing stillness. The air shifted, crackling, as he landed silently behind me. His sheer presence saturated the small space, shrinking it, charging it. Making it infinitely more dangerous.

"The training master reported an abrupt departure," his voice rumbled, low and rough-edged, vibrating through the stone beneath my feet.

I was still facing out. "I needed space." My voice was tight, brittle.

He moved closer. He didn't walk. He stalked. Each step was measured, deliberate, closing the distance until he stood beside me. His heat rolled off him in waves, scorching the air, raising gooseflesh despite the burn.

He was close enough to feel the thrum of his power. I finally risked a glance. Dark scales drank the dying light, revealing pulsing fiery undertones. His eyes—molten gold, ancient fire, impossible to read— were fixed on me with an intensity that kicked my pulse into a frantic, traitorous rhythm.

He held something. Dark leather, glinting alloy. Intricate straps. Sized for ... me.

My throat went dry. "What is that?" The question was a croak.

"Yours," he stated simply, extending it. It was a flight harness. The complex arrangement dangled between us, heavy with implication. Exquisite craftsmanship. Supple, dark leather, lightweight metal buckles gleaming dully. Reinforced seams, adjustable clasps.

"To secure you," he explained, his voice dropping, roughening further. "Against falling. But it allows ... adjustment. Freedom. Mid-flight."

My fingers reached, ghosting over the cool leather, the precise stitching. Hours of work. Days.

For me. A lump formed in my throat, thick and painful.

This wasn't just gear. It was a statement. A claim.

"This is ..." The words caught, strangled. My voice shook. It felt like a betrayal. "You shouldn't have."

"You deserve sanctuary. Safety." His words cut through my attempt at deflection, raw and absolute. The lack of his usual guarded control stripped me bare. "This," he gestured with the harness, "is merely ... practical."

Practical. As if the word could mask the sheer possessive weight of the gesture. As if it wasn't a promise forged in leather and steel.

"Permit me," he rumbled, less a question, more a quiet command that sent a fresh tide of heat crashing through me.

Hesitation warred with a desperate, aching need to accept. Not just the harness. All of it. The dangerous connection. The fragile sense of belonging he offered.

"Alright," I breathed, the word barely audible. But his sharp intake of breath, the slight flare of his nostrils, told me he'd heard the surrender beneath it.

He moved behind me. Close. Too close. His presence enveloped me, overwhelming my senses. I lifted my arms stiffly, allowing him to slide the harness over my head, settling it onto my shoulders. His claws, usually weapons, moved with shocking precision, adjusting straps, securing buckles. Each touch was careful. Electric. The backs of his scaled fingers brushed my ribs as he tightened a side strap. A violent shiver wracked my frame.

"Too tight?" The question was a low growl, missing the cause entirely.

I shook my head, unable to trust my voice. His hands paused at my waist, fingers splayed, heat searing through my shirt. Lingering. Branding me. When he finally moved around to face me, checking the front fastenings, the look in his eyes gutted me.

Hunger. Stark. Unfiltered. A predator's assessment barely leashed by iron control. But beneath it, something deeper, more terrifying. A profound vulnerability mirrored in raw possessiveness.

"It fits," he murmured, his gaze sweeping down the harness, then locking onto mine.

His knuckles brushed the sensitive skin just above my collarbone as he adjusted one last strap. Sparks ignited along my nerve pathways. I sucked in a shaky breath, hyperaware of the scant inches separating us, the furnace of his body, the way my own pulsed in response.

"Thank you." The whisper was rough, inadequate. My heart hammered against the confines of the harness, a frantic drumbeat of warning and anticipation. "It's ... intricate work."

He rumbled low and deep. It was satisfaction. Possession. Power. "There is more I would give you," he stated, the words a low promise, heavy with unspoken meaning. "So much more, *vrakasha*."

I exhaled, the sound ragged. Each step deeper into this—into him—shredded the careful defenses I'd rebuilt stone by painful stone.

But when his hand lifted, calloused thumb tracing a feather-light path along my cheekbone, the jolt short-circuited thought. Only this moment. Only the searing heat of what burned between us, consuming everything else.

"I heard them," I blurted, the words escaping before I could cage them. "In the training pit. The Elder. About the Council. That you're ..." The words caught. Risking everything. For me.

His expression tightened, a flicker of granite, then softened fractionally as he searched my face. "Always," he confirmed. The single word resonated like a vow hammered into stone. "Without reservation."

The weight of it—the political firestorm, the danger he courted—threatened to suffocate me.

"They're right," I whispered, the fear raw, exposed. "This is dangerous. What we ... this connection. It's changing things."

"Yes." The agreement was a deep growl, felt more than heard, vibrating against my bones. "It is."

His hand slid from my cheek, cupping the back of my neck, fingers tangling in the short strands of my hair. The immense strength held in check, the careful restraint costing him visible effort—that was more seductive, more terrifying, than any overt force.

"I don't know how," I admitted, the vulnerability ripped from me, leaving me exposed. "How to navigate this. Be what you need. What your people demand."

"I require only you," he countered, leaning closer, his breath a hot caress against my lips. The scent of him filled my head. "As you are. Fierce. Defiant." His eyes burned into mine. "Mine."

Mine.

It slammed into me, a brand seared onto my soul. Every instinct screamed danger, flight. But a deeper, traitorous pulse flared low in my belly, a hunger answering his own.

The harness seemed to tighten as I dragged in another shaky breath, a physical reminder of his claim. Tentatively, I reached up, fingers tracing the hard, unyielding line of his jaw. Cool, smooth scales under my touch. Alien. Intoxicating.

The chasm between our worlds felt vast, insurmountable. Yet the current arcing between us ignored it all, raw and undeniable. Living lightning.

I surrendered. Not softly. But like yielding to a gravity too strong to fight. Whatever this was, wherever it dragged us—down into fire or up into the lethal beauty of his sky—there was no turning back now.

For tonight, I would fall.

THE HARNESS SAT tight on her body. Leather and steel. A claim. I'd spent hours measuring, cutting, stitching it just for her. It was my mark on her skin. Her fingers traced the buckles, eyes wide. Was it gratitude? Maybe. Uncertainty? Sure. But something else pulsed under it all.

"It's good work," she murmured, her voice almost lost to the wind whistling outside. Those dark eyes met mine. They were questioning, but defiant too. "I've never had anything made just for me. Not like this."

Pride surged hot. It was primal. Fierce. "The first," I said, my voice rough. My tail swept the stone floor behind me, restless. I couldn't keep it still.

The harness showed off the hard lines of her body—a warrior's body, built for killing. It was different from our females, but just as dangerous. Just as fucking magnificent. Thinking about flying with her, feeling her strapped against me while we cut through Volcaryth's winds ... heat pooled low in my gut.

She glanced at the darkening sky, then back at me. Her chin lifted a fraction. She took a deep breath. A decision made, clear as a shout.

"Not tonight," she said. Her voice was soft, but final. "The flight, I mean." Her fingers tested a strap. "But I want to keep wearing this. For now."

Right. Not the sky. Something else. The air between us grew thick, heavy.

I held out my hand, scaled palm up. "Come."

For a second, I thought she'd back off. She would remember the Council, the Temple priests bitching about us, the fucking gap between our kinds. Instead, her smaller hand slid into mine. Her fingers curled tight against my scales. Solid.

"Lead the way, Stone Fist."

I led her through the stone corridors. I felt every stare from the warriors we passed, heard every hissed whisper. Let them look. Let them fucking see. My wings shifted, half-opening behind her. A warning.

Try me.

The siege quarters felt smaller with her inside.

Closer. The heat crystals pulsed low, throwing her shadow long on the floor. I slammed the door shut, the clicks echoing my hammering pulse. Locked us in.

When I turned, she stood near the sleeping platform, fingers trailing over the silks. The harness emphasized her shoulders, the curve of her hip. Shadows clung to her collarbones, her throat. Her scent—human sweat and something else, something just *her*—filled the small space. It wrapped around me, tightened my throat, made my cock stir.

"Hawk," I rasped. My voice sounded like rocks grinding together. I kept my distance. Gave her space. Prayed she wouldn't take it.

She met my eyes, steady. In the low light, they looked black. Watching me. Thinking. Her tongue darted out, wetting her lips. Was it nerves? Or was she doing it on purpose? Didn't matter. It broke something inside me.

"I'm not good at this," she breathed. "This thing between us."

"Neither am I," I admitted, stepping closer. Couldn't help it. I was drawn like metal to a lodestone. "But I know what I feel."

Her breath hitched. "What's that?"

I closed the gap. Slow. Deliberate. My hand

lifted, cupped her cheek. Careful. Gentle. Her skin felt too smooth against my rough scales. Warm. Alive.

"Mine," I growled. The word ripped out, raw possession. Nothing else mattered.

My tail snaked around her waist. A living strap holding her to me. Even through the clothes, the contact burned. She sucked in a sharp breath. Her pulse jumped under my fingers. Every reaction was a victory.

Her hands came up to my chest. I tensed, waiting for her to push me away. Instead, her palms pressed flat against my scales. Exploring. Heat flared where she touched.

"This should scare me," she whispered, fingers tracing the edge of a scale.

"Does it?" My voice dropped lower until it was rumbling.

"Yes." There was a pause. Her eyes lifted. Defiant. Vulnerable. "No."

I traced her jaw with my thumb. Felt her pulse leap. "I wouldn't cage you, *vrakasha*. Just ... let me keep you safe."

Something in her eyes softened. Gave way. That broke the last of my control.

I bent my head, closing the final inch, and

claimed her mouth. There was no hesitation this time. Hunger. Need. She tasted of water, of human heat, of something that made my tongue tingle and my fangs ache.

Her mouth answered mine, turning the kiss rougher. Her hands slid up my neck, fingers digging into the sensitive spot where scales met hide. Fire shot through me. A low growl vibrated from my throat into her mouth.

My tail tightened, then slid lower. It went over the curve of her hip, down the strength of her thigh. She gasped against my lips, arching into the touch. Each reaction pushed me further. My hands roamed her back, learning the shape of her through cloth and leather.

"Khorlar," she murmured, the sound husky. It was liquid fire in my veins.

I shuffled backward, pulling her toward the sleeping platform. Didn't want to break contact, not even for a second. Her hands got bolder. They traced the ridges on my chest, found the sensitive edges of my scales. Her nails scraped lightly over my stomach. Pleasure ripped through me, sharp and sudden.

"Show me," she demanded, eyes burning in the dim light. "How to touch you."

The order, so fucking bold, cracked something

deep inside. My control—years of discipline, battle—frayed. Gone.

"Everything," I admitted, my voice thick. I cupped the back of her neck, felt the short silk of her hair. "But here ..." I guided her hand to the base of my wing, where the scales were thin. "And here ..." Under my jaw, where hide was softer.

Her touch grew bolder. Each stroke sent jolts through me. The heat between us wasn't just mine anymore. It poured off her. Her scent thickened. Rich with a desire I knew even without being human.

We hit the sleeping platform. I let her guide our fall onto the silks, wings flaring to soften the landing. She landed on top of me. Her weight, solid and real, drew a satisfied rumble from my chest. Her surprised laugh—sharp, precious—rumbled against my scales.

"Sorry," she said, but she was grinning. "Still getting used to ... all this." She waved a hand vaguely at my wings, my tail. Me.

I traced her smile with my thumb. Watched the firelight on her face. "Me too, *vrakasha*. You break every rule."

My honesty seemed to catch her off guard. Her face shifted—unguarded, open—just for a second.

Then she lowered her mouth to mine again, stealing my breath.

Her fingers found the buckles on my battle harness. Fumbled a little. I helped her, shedding the armor fast. Each piece hitting the floor made me more aware of her. Her scent. Her heat. The way her breath hitched when my bare scales met the air.

"Can I?" I asked. My fingers hovered near her shirt.

She nodded. Sharp. Quick.

I moved carefully. My claws could rip this flimsy stuff easily, and I did, cutting her shirt away around my gift. The harness I'd made was still there. Leather on bare skin. Possessive heat flared in me. Mine.

"Leave it," she ordered, seeing me reach for the buckles. "I like how it feels."

Fuck. That almost broke me. My free hand clenched the silk bedding, claws sinking deep. I was fighting for control.

Her pants came next. Gone. Leaving her in just the harness and some light wraps underneath. Leather against skin. Firelight on her curves, in the hollows. An image burned into my brain.

Forever.

"Your turn," she challenged. Her fingers went to the ties on my own pants.

I helped her. Lifted my hips. Let her strip the last barrier away. She sucked in a sharp breath when my cock sprang free, hard and flushed. She stared. There was no shame. Her eyes tracked the thick length, the obsidian scales giving way to pulsing flesh, the slick bead of need at the tip.

"Yes," she murmured. Curiosity mixed with something else. Hunger. "Please."

Her fingers touched me. Feather-light. Exploring. A growl tore from my throat. My hips bucked. Her eyes widened, not with fear, but satisfaction. Fierce. Matching mine.

"Show me," she repeated.

I guided her hand. Showed her the pressure, the rhythm. Her fingers—smaller, smoother than any Drakarn female's—on my sensitive flesh. It was almost too much. She bent her head. Her tongue flicked out, tasted the head of my cock. My control shattered. Gone.

With a snarl, I flipped her. Rolled her underneath me. Careful, but fast. Her startled gasp turned into a moan when my mouth found the pulse beating fast in her throat. I tasted my way down her body. Learned her sounds. Where she sighed. Where she gasped. Where a light scrape of my fang made her curse and arch her spine.

My tail slid between her thighs. Found her heat. Teased the sensitive flesh there. She was wet. Ready. Her body was honest. Her scent—human musk, mixed with pure *Hawk*—drove me wild.

"Please," she breathed. Raw. Needy.

I lifted my head from her breast. Met her eyes. "Tell me what you want."

"You," she answered. There was no hesitation. She was reaching for me. "Inside me. Now."

The demand. It was straightforward. Fierce. Just like her. No games. Just need. Matching mine.

I positioned myself between her thighs. My cock ached. Needed to claim her. Possess her. But deeper than that ... I wanted to please her. Worship her. Make this mean something.

"Look at me," I commanded. Needed to see her eyes when I took her.

Dark eyes met mine. Gold fire reflected in them. A connection deeper than skin. I pushed forward. Slow. Breaching her entrance. Fuck, she was tight. Slick heat gripped my cock. Inch by slow inch, I filled her. Her breath came in short, sharp pants. Her fingers dug into my shoulders, right where scales met softer skin.

When I was buried deep inside, I stopped. Fought the urge to slam into her. Claim her hard.

Her inner muscles fluttered around me. Tightening. Adjusting. I dropped my forehead to hers. Breathed her in. Let her scent fill me, calm the fire threatening to burn me up.

"Move," she finally whispered. It was barely audible. "Please, Khorlar. Move."

I obeyed. Pulled back almost all the way, then sank deep again. The drag. The glide. The friction. A groan ripped from my chest. Her answering moan, her legs locking around my waist, pulling me deeper —nothing had ever felt like this.

We found a rhythm. Old as time, but new. Her hands explored my back, my sides. Found places that sent shocks straight to my cock. My tail coiled around her thigh, pulsing with my thrusts. Another connection. Another claim.

"Yes," she gasped, head thrown back. Throat exposed. "Right there."

I changed my angle. Pushed deeper. Hit a spot that made her eyes fly wide, her breath catch. Seeing her like that—flushed, desperate, the harness framing her panting chest—broke the last of my restraint. My pace quickened. Each thrust pounding into her. A claim.

Mine. Mine. Mine.

Her climax hit her hard. Her body arched off the

silks, muscles clamping down on my cock in tight pulses. Trying to pull me over the edge with her. She cried out, raw and wild. Her nails dug into my scales.

"Khorlar," she gasped, eyes wide, unfocused. "God, Khorlar ..."

My name on her lips. Broken. Fucking reverent. It shattered everything. My release tore through me like lava. Burning hot. I buried my face in her neck, breathing her in as I pumped my seed deep inside her. Marking her. Filling her.

We collapsed. Tangled in damp sheets. Sweat. Sex. My tail draped over her leg. Protective. I didn't want to let go. Our breathing slowed. Hearts stopped hammering.

In the quiet, I pulled her closer. One wing half-covered her. She didn't fight it. Her smaller body fit against mine. It was like she was made for it. The thought sent a fresh wave of possession through me. And something else. Tender. An ache under my ribs.

"I never expected this," I admitted. My voice was rough. Thick with feeling. "You. What you are to me."

She tilted her head. Looked at me with those eyes that saw too damn much. "And what's that?"

I traced her cheek. Her soft skin. The strength

underneath. "Everything," I answered. It was simple. True. "Honor. Purpose. Home."

Something flickered in her eyes—fear, maybe wonder—gone too fast. Then her face softened. Just a little. She leaned up, pressed her lips to the scales over my heart.

"Whatever this is ... it scares me how much I need it."

Her honesty hit me harder than any blade. I tightened my hold. Her heartbeat, steady against my chest. No battle won ever felt like this. This wasn't surrender. It was ... a meeting. Equals.

"Sleep, *vrakasha*," I rumbled, stroking her short hair.

She made a soft sound. Was it protest? Agreement? But her body relaxed against mine. In the dim glow of the heat crystals, her safe in my arms, I finally admitted the truth. The one burning me up since I first smelled her.

She was mine. I was hers. And I'd tear apart anyone—Council, Temple, Ignarath himself—who tried to touch what we were building.

As she drifted off, her breathing evening out, one last truth settled deep in my bones. It was as hard as stone.

I would burn the world to ash before I let her go.

LEATHER BIT INTO MY SHOULDERS. It wasn't pain, just pressure—a constant, chafing reminder of the harness. A reminder of him.

I'd slept in the damned thing.

My fingers traced the tight, intricate stitching—his work—as I walked. Hours spent on it. For me. The implications sent a dizzying warmth flooding my veins, unwelcome and undeniable.

"You're a fool," I muttered, forcing my boots faster over the stone. Ahead, heat crystals embedded in the rock ceiling pulsed, throwing waves of dull orange light that painted my shadow long and skeletal on the wall. It rippled, distorted as I moved. It was unrecognizable.

Like me.

Khorlar's weight seemed to press down even

now, settling heavy. His scent clung to my skin despite scrubbing. His taste, sharp and metallic, still coated my tongue. The memory of rough scales scraping mine, the furnace heat of his body, the molten gold intensity of his eyes ... those were memories that wouldn't fade.

Mine.

It was his claim. A brand seared into my mind. What terrified me more was the treacherous part of me that wanted it.

Ahead, the corridor opened into the central chamber. Voices drifted out—Selene's measured calm, a counterpoint to Eden's rapid-fire chatter. This was home base. My people. The anchor I needed against the current threatening to pull me under.

I paused just inside the threshold, scanning. It was habit. I assessed the room. Eden's chaotic sprawl of tech—scavenged guts of our transport gleaming under the heat crystals. Kaiya was hunched over glowing samples, muttering something I didn't understand. Selene, efficient as ever, was sorting medical supplies near the far wall.

"Look who decided to grace us," Lexa called out, spotting me. Her grin was sharp, all teeth, barely reaching her eyes. "Enjoying your private suite while the rest of us slum it?"

The words landed like tiny darts. I forced my own smile, thin as cracked ice. "Hardly a five-star resort."

Selene looked up then, her gaze sweeping over me, pausing fractionally on the harness visible beneath my open jacket. That quiet, assessing stare missed nothing. Understanding flickered there. Or maybe pity. Worse.

"New gear?" she asked, her voice soft. It was too soft.

Heat flared up my neck, hot and prickly. "A flight harness." I aimed for casual, landed somewhere near a cornered animal.

"Custom?" Selene's hands stilled over a roll of bandages. "Khorlar's work?"

Damn it. "How—"

"The stitching," she cut me off smoothly. "Vyne mentioned warriors develop unique patterns. Like a signature."

Perfect. It was a brand. My face burned. "It's ... practical."

"Of course." Her smile was infuriatingly gentle. There was no judgment, just quiet knowledge. Worse than any accusation.

"Vega?" I asked, needing to shift the focus off me. Off the harness. Off him. "Has anyone seen her lately?"

Eden glanced up, pushing stray wires aside. "She said she was going to the lower passageways. She said something about checking exits."

A cold fist clenched in my gut. Vega alone. Near potential escape routes. After our fight. After her obsession with finding other survivors.

"Kira and Reika?" The question felt tight in my throat.

Lexa frowned. "I haven't seen Kira since yesterday."

Yesterday? The fist tightened.

"She asked Vyne for border territory maps," Selene added, her movements slowing, concern finally showing in the set of her shoulders.

Alarm bells started ringing loud in my head. "You've gotta be fucking kidding me." I breathed the words. The pieces slammed together. Ugly. Sharp.

"You don't think—" Selene started.

The door crashed open. It was Vega. Her chest heaving, face stark white under the orange glow. Wild panic in her eyes. Locked on mine.

"Kira's gone." She was panting. Raw. "I searched

everywhere. The training grounds. The mess. Even the freaking temple courtyard. Gone."

Silence crushed us. It was heavy. Suffocating. Eden's tools clattered against the table, the sound sharp in the stillness. Lexa swore.

"When?" My voice felt distant, scraped raw.

"Last night." Vega's voice frayed at the edges. "She packed supplies. Weapons."

Selene whispered it, the awful truth dawning. "Her sister."

"Ignarath *rumors*," I finished, ice spreading through my veins. The infirmary. My words. My focus on Khorlar. Driving her away. "She went after her." Goddamn it. "Because you—" Now was *not* the time for a fight.

"We go. Now." Vega's hand flashed to the knife at her hip. Primal instinct. "Before the trail vanishes."

"Hold up," I snapped, hands raised. Defensive. Trying to regain control I didn't feel. "We need a fucking plan. Backup." How many times did I have to say this?

Vega's eyes blazed. "Backup? Your lizard man? The Council scheming to trade us like cattle?"

"We can't just storm Ignarath territory!" The words ripped out, raw with frustration and fear. "Not after that scout nearly gutted me!"

"While we debate strategy, Kira's out there!" Vega shot back, desperation cracking her voice. "Captured. Or worse."

"Or dead," Lexa added, her voice flat. Brutal truth.

Silence fell again, thick with unspoken fears.

"Tell Darrokar," Selene urged, her calm a frayed lifeline in the rising panic. "Khorlar. Vyne. Rath. All of them. They're on our side. They know the terrain—"

"There's no time!" Vega slashed the air with her hand. "And no guarantee they'd help. Not with politics poisoning everything."

She wasn't necessarily wrong. The fractures in the Council. The Temple pressure. Khorlar ... compromised. Because of me.

But four of us were mated to Drakarn now. That had to count for something. They wouldn't just abandon us.

My hand scrubbed down my face, grit stinging my eyes. Duty. Loyalty. Responsibility. A crushing weight, stealing the air from my lungs.

"You need gear," I forced out, the word tasting like ash. Hating the compromise. Hating myself. "Scout *only*. Find her trail. That's it. No engagement.

Then you report back." If we had actionable intel, someone would help. I had to believe that.

Relief flooded Vega's face. Too fast. Too absolute. "Thank you."

"Any trouble," I warned, pinning her with my gaze, "any hint—you come straight back. We get Khorlar. Darrokar. Whatever it takes."

"Agreed." I didn't believe her. And a big part of me thought I should go with her. Selene was looking worried, and no doubt word of this would get to the Drakarn soon enough.

"Rations," Lexa said, already moving. "Water."

Twenty minutes felt like an hour etched in stone. Vega was in light armor salvaged from the crash. She had a knife, enough water for a day, and as much information as we could give her.

This was a huge mistake.

Still, I led the way to one of the easier to access exits.

The lower corridors descended into deeper shadow. Heat crystals were sparse there, leaving stretches of near-total blackness between pools of sullen light. Our boots echoed, too loud in the quiet. The stone walls felt rough, damp under my questing fingers. Vega moved with tense certainty, weaving through the passages like she owned them. She knew these ways. Too well.

"You've been down here before," I accused, voice low.

She didn't look back. "I've done some contingency planning." Her silhouette was rigid in the gloom ahead.

"For you and Kira doing something stupid?"

A humorless twist of her lips was barely visible. "Or you."

The passage narrowed again, the ceiling pressing down, stealing air. Breathing felt tight. We moved by touch, fingers scraping rough-hewn stone. I wanted to find this exit and watch her go, assure myself that at least the first part of this harebrained scheme would work.

Then I was running back and telling Khorlar everything. Vega would hate me for it, but I couldn't see another way.

A shift in the shadows ahead. It was larger than human. Dense. Solid.

Vega surged forward, hope making her reckless. "Kira?" She rounded the blind corner before I could grab her.

"Vega, wait!" I hissed, lunging after her, the

harness cinching tight across my ribs as I ran. Another bend and—

Solid impact. It was Vega's back. Rigid. Frozen.

She was staring into the dark filling the narrow passage. Filling it completely.

I didn't need to see to know who it was.

Khorlar.

Light flared around him, a portable heat crystal almost blinding for a moment.

His wings were folded impossibly tight in the confined space, gray scales absorbing the faint, distant light like a void. His heat radiated out, a physical wave washing over us, making the air shimmer. His eyes burned, molten gold embers in the gloom, locking onto me. Fixing on the gear. The barely concealed weapons. The intent was clear on my face.

His nostrils flared, sampling the air—our sweat, our fear, our purpose.

Something shifted behind those eyes. It was something cold. Terrible.

"Going somewhere, *vrakasha?*"

His voice. Oh gods. It wasn't loud. Low. A deep rumble that pulsed through the stone floor, up my legs, into my teeth. Eerily calm. Deadly calm.

The world compressed. Just us three. Vega was

vibrating with desperate tension beside me. Khorlar was radiating barely leashed fury before us, a physical pressure against my skin. And me. I was impaled between them.

"Kira," I managed to say, lifting my chin, forcing the word out past the constriction in my throat. "She's missing." The words were all wrong, but nothing could be right, not right now.

His gaze flicked to Vega, dismissive, then snapped back to me. It was hard. Accusing. "And you chose not to inform me."

It was not a question. A blade twisting slow and deep.

"There was no time," Vega spat, stepping forward instinctively, putting herself slightly between us. "She could be all the way to—"

"And you intended to follow?" Khorlar cut her off, the calm cracking like ice under pressure. His voice dropped lower, harsher, scraping like stone on stone. Scales rippled along his neck and shoulders, catching faint highlights. "Into oblivion?"

"Just scouting," I tried, the lie pathetic and thin on my tongue. Useless.

His jaw clenched, the sound audible in the sudden, ringing silence. It was sharp. "Lies. Do. Not. Suit. You. Hawk."

My real name. Not the intimate vrakasha. A slap. It was harder than any physical blow. My breath hitched.

"You don't—" I started, desperate.

"No?" His tail slammed against the stone wall behind him.

CRACK.

The sound echoed like a gunshot in the tight space, making me flinch.

"Explain, then. Why my mate prepares to abandon our quarters? To flee into enemy territory? Without a word?"

Mate.

The word detonated in the space between us. Burning heat flooded my face. Vega's sharp intake of breath beside me. Exposed. Raw. Laid bare under that burning gold stare.

"Your mate doesn't need permission," Vega snarled, moving fully in front of me now. Protective. Reckless. Facing down a storm. "She's not property."

"Vega—" My warning died in my throat.

Too late. The leash snapped.

A growl ripped from Khorlar's chest, a subterranean vibration shaking the air, the rock, my bones. His wings flared wide, powerful muscles bunching, the sharp edges scraping stone, boxing us in further.

Scales darkened, shifting like storm clouds gathering for violence. The air grew thick with his scent, sharp ozone and raw, unrestrained fury.

"You know *nothing*," he snarled, fangs flashing white against black scales in the dimness. "Nothing of our bond. Nothing of what waits beyond these borders. You push her toward death and call it loyalty?"

"We're saving a life!" Vega yelled back, defiant, but her hand trembled near her knife.

"By sacrificing two more?" His voice dropped again, silk over razors, terrifying in its softness. "The Ignarath do not capture, little fool. They erase. And you ..." His burning gaze found me again, slicing through Vega's defiance. The fury underneath bled raw pain. Hurt. Betrayal. "You would throw away everything? Everything we are building? Everything you are to me?"

The harness felt like iron bands now, crushing my ribs, stealing my breath. His gift. His claim. Pressed against my heart while I stood ready to shatter his trust.

"I wasn't ..." How could I even say it? Did it even matter? "She's my responsibility. My people."

Something fractured in his gaze then. It shattered like breaking obsidian. "And what am I?"

The question struck like a physical blow, knocking the air from my lungs. Breathless. What was he? Captor. Protector. Ally. Lover. Enemy? The lines blurred into an unbearable knot tightening deep inside me.

"We're wasting time!" Vega hissed, desperate, glancing nervously down the dark corridor behind us. "Kira—"

Khorlar didn't look away from me. He didn't blink. He was waiting. Demanding an answer I didn't have. Couldn't give. The silence stretched, suffocating, filled with the weight of everything broken between us.

"Please," I choked out, unsure what I begged for. Mercy? Understanding? Release?

His face became stone. Scales pulled taut over bone. Decision hardening his eyes into impenetrable gold shields.

"You're not going anywhere," he declared, voice absolute. Final. Like rock grinding against rock. "Not alone. Not like this."

Vega tensed beside me, her hand tightening on her knife hilt. She was ready to fight a force of nature.

Fear, cold and sharp, pierced through me. Not

for me. For Vega. For him. For the explosion waiting to happen in this suffocatingly small space.

And me, the catalyst, caught in the middle. Torn. Bleeding.

THE AIR THICKENED WITH BETRAYAL. It coiled in my gut, hot and corrosive as the lava rivers that cut through Volcaryth. Rage wasn't a strong enough word. This was immolation, a scorching away of everything but the raw, primal wound of seeing her stand there.

My mate.

She was poised for escape in the claustrophobic confines of the tunnel. Weapons barely concealed beneath the harness—my harness, the one I'd fitted to the curve of her waist, the slope of her shoulders. The scent of her, usually a balm to my senses, was now laced with the sharp tang of defiance, of fear, and something else ... determination. It scraped against my insides. Beside her, the other human female, Vega, vibrated with a nervous energy that set my teeth on edge, her eyes glittering like shards of ice.

"You will not pass," I repeated. The words were stone, each syllable chipped from the mountain of fury building inside me. The calm in my voice was a thin crust over magma. "Not alone. Not like this."

Vega's hand spasmed on her blade hilt. It was a pathetic gesture. A piece of sharpened metal against a warrior born of fire and stone? Against me? Nothing stood between me and my mate.

"You don't command us," Vega spat, taking a half-step forward, bristling like a cornered ground-rat. "Kira is out there—"

"I don't give a molten damn about Kira!" The control snapped. My voice ripped through the confined space. My wings flared, the tips scraping stone, sending showers of grit raining down. The movement was pure territorial aggression. "My concern is her." I jabbed a clawed finger toward Hawk. "My mate. Who apparently thinks nothing of shattering our bond, of walking into the jaws of the Ignarath for a reckless chase!"

Hawk flinched, but her shoulders squared under the harness. That damned harness.

"That's enough," she snapped. She moved then, stepping fluidly between me and Vega. She was always the shield. Even now, when I felt like the one being attacked. "This isn't about us. Kira is missing. Ignarath territory is the most likely place. We have to look."

"And your plan?" The word dripped contempt. "Sneak out like rock-worms tunneling in the dark? Offer yourselves up on Ignarath blades?"

"Vega was going to scout," she insisted, but her gaze slid away for a fraction of a second. Was she lying? If she didn't intend to leave, why was she down here with Vega?

"Scout," I echoed, the sound a low growl rumbling from my chest. "Into their hunting grounds. After one of them nearly gutted you. After everything I told you about the dangers."

Vega made a noise of pure frustration. "There's no time! While you two posture—"

"Vega." Hawk's command was quiet but absolute, cutting off the other human. She didn't look away from me. "Give us a moment."

Vega bristled, clearly wanting to argue, but Hawk's stillness held her. With a final glare poisoned with dislike, she retreated around the bend, out of sight but not, I knew, out of earshot.

Silence descended, heavy and charged. It pulsed between us, thick with unspoken wounds, with anger that felt dangerously close to grief. The stone walls seemed to press closer, amplifying the frantic beat of my own heart against my ribs.

Then, she moved. She did not retreat. She moved toward me.

Two strides. That's all it took to close the space until mere inches separated us. I could feel the warmth radiating from her skin, smell the unique blend of human and the faint metallic tang of the Scalvaris air clinging to her clothes. That scent ... gods, it still undid me.

"I wasn't leaving you," she said, her voice a low vibration, pitched just for me, barely audible above the hum of the geothermal currents below. The words slammed into me, cracking the icy shell of my fury. "I wouldn't. Not like that."

My throat felt constricted, tight as a closing fist. "How can I believe that?" The worders were rough, torn from me.

"Because you know me," she said, her gaze holding mine, fierce and unwavering. "I was going to come find you as soon as I was sure Vega left safely. I wanted to find you before. But I'm being torn in two. I can't leave my people behind, Khorlar. Any more than you could leave yours."

The truth of it stung, a bitter venom. Her loyalty.

It was one of the first things that had drawn me, that core of unyielding strength. But seeing it turned away from me, even for a noble cause ... it felt like betrayal all the same.

"We do this properly," I snarled, the sound softening despite myself, the anger warring with a desperate need to keep her close, safe. "Together. With warriors. With a plan. Not ... this." I waved a hand, dismissing her ill-conceived mission. "This is suicide."

"Speed is crucial," she pressed, sensing the shift in me. "We need search teams. If Kira left—and I think she did, looking for her sister—she'd use the eastern tunnels. They're less watched."

"And if Ignarath took her?" The thought was a knife to the gut. Not for the missing human herself, but for the implications. Escalation. War. And Hawk ... Hawk right in the middle of it.

"Then finding her fast is even more critical," she replied, her expression hardening. "We move now, Khorlar. Please."

I looked down at her, this impossible female. She was fragile and fierce, human and yet ... mine. She had shattered my world, rearranged my priorities, burrowed under my scales in a way nothing else ever had.

"Together," I repeated, the word a vow, a command. "You stay within my sight. Always."

Relief washed over her face, softening the tense lines around her eyes. "Yes."

I turned, folding my wings tight to navigate the passage. The lingering scent of her fear and determination clung to the air. "Call your friend," I ordered, my voice regaining its edge. "We gather the warriors."

———

The muster was a controlled storm of movement and low commands. Darrokar orchestrated the deployment with chilling efficiency. Two teams. Vyne and Selene would lead the search within Scalvaris's labyrinthine lower levels. Zarvash, Ryvik, myself, Hawk, and Vega would take the skies beyond the eastern border with a contingent of young warriors.

"The Ignarath will view this as aggression," Darrokar warned, his voice a low rumble beneath the clang of weapons checks. His obsidian eyes flicked from me to Hawk, standing resolute at my side, strapped into the flight harness. "Exercise caution. Stick to the objective."

I gave a curt nod. "Find the human. Return. Nothing else."

"See that you do, Stone Fist." His gaze lingered on Hawk for a heartbeat longer than necessary, a silent reminder of the precarious balance we maintained. "The Council convenes at dawn. I expect all humans accounted for."

Failure wasn't merely inconvenient; it could shatter the balance of power.

I pushed the political maneuvering aside. It was useless. My focus narrowed to the female beside me. "Ready?" I turned, my claws automatically checking the harness buckles, the tension of the straps across her body. My fingers brushed the worn leather, the brief contact sending a familiar, possessive heat through my veins, momentarily banking the fires of my earlier anger.

"Not my first flight clinging to your grumpy ass," she murmured, the words meant only for me. It was a weak jest, undermined by the worry tightening her eyes.

I growled deep. "Focus, *vrakasha*. We'll find your friend. Then we address ... other matters."

The eastern launch plateau gaped open to the night, a wide shelf carved into the mountain, slick with volcanic glass. I secured Hawk against my chest, her back pressed firmly against me, the harness a tangible link between us. Her muscles were coiled tight, but she leaned into my strength, a silent acknowledgment of trust that eased something brittle inside me.

Zarvash stood poised nearby, Vega similarly secured with a makeshift harness. The bronze warrior's face was a mask of grim calculation. "Eastern quadrant," he stated, his claw indicating the obsidian plains stretching towards the jagged silhouette of Ignarath territory. "Outer marker first, spiral pattern."

I nodded, scanning the darkness. "The trail is fresh. We'll find her."

Then, we leaped, our warriors flanked out behind us.

The air punched the breath from my lungs, a brutal, exhilarating shock. I felt Hawk gasp, her hands instinctively tightening on the forearm I banded across her middle. Then, as my wings caught the powerful thermal updrafts, biting into the air, her grip eased fractionally. It was not fear. It was anticipation. Even now, danger snapping at our heels, the sheer act of flight thrilled her. Stubborn female.

Beneath us, the world transformed into a nightmare landscape painted in blacks and smoldering reds by the twin setting suns. Rivers of lava pulsed like the planet's arteries, cutting glowing paths across the dark plains. And far ahead, the Crystal Mountains loomed, radiating menace—Ignarath lands.

We flew low and fast, skimming the tortured earth, eyes scanning, senses straining. The wind brought only the taste of sulfur and cold stone, no human scent, no sign. Hope began to bleed away, replaced by a cold certainty.

Then—a flicker. Near the eastern tunnel mouth, close to the jagged edge of our territory. Movement, unnatural against the static backdrop of rock. I banked sharply, the maneuver shearing wind, feeling Hawk tense as she spotted it simultaneously.

"There," her voice was tight, strained against the rush of air. "By that spire."

My eyes narrowed, piercing the gloom. Figures huddled in the deep shadows cast by the massive rock formation. Not Ignarath; their movements lacked the predatory fluidity. And the robes ... robes the color of sickly sulfur blooms. Yellow.

A cold fist clenched in my gut. Temple acolytes. Karyseth's insidious flock.

"Zarvash," I called, the wind snatching at the name. He was already altering course, the strategist's mind processing the scene as swiftly as mine.

We descended in a tightening spiral, landing carefully, the impact of our talons muffled by dust. I kept Hawk bound to me, my protective instincts screaming, refusing to release her into this unknown.

The scene resolved. Three humans sprawled on the black ground, limp, vulnerable. Kira. The rescued one, Reika. Another I didn't recognize, possibly the doctor Rachel. And surrounding them, six acolytes, their yellow robes unnervingly bright in the dying light. No obvious weapons, but their hands ... their hands shimmered faintly with the unsettling energy of their so-called Sacred Flame. Temple magic. Disciplines I neither trusted nor understood.

"What in the hells?" Hawk breathed against my back, her body rigid.

"Let me down," she demanded, her voice low, urgent, vibrating against my scales. "Khorlar. Release the harness. Now."

"No," I growled, my grip tightening reflexively. "We assess first. This smells wrong."

"Those are my people!" she hissed, beginning to struggle, straining against the harness. "Damn it, Khorlar, let me—"

A flicker of movement high above. On the ridge line overlooking the spire. Dark shapes detaching themselves from the rock face, wings unfolding against the blood-streaked sky. Silhouettes sharp with menace. Crimson streaks marking their wings.

Ignarath.

"A trap." The word ripped from my throat, cold dread mixing with boiling rage. I shoved Hawk behind my legs as I unlatched the harness with brutal speed. "Zarvash!"

The bronze warrior was already reacting, thrusting Vega towards us as his blade sang free of its sheath. "Six," he snapped, eyes tracking the descent. "Airborne. Coming in hot."

The acolytes looked up, their expressions shifting from grim purpose to something akin to ... satisfaction? Then surprise, as they registered us. One, a female marked with silver scales, stepped forward.

"The Temple claims these trespassers," her voice rang out, surprisingly carrying over the rising wind. "By Sacred Flame and Karyseth's will."

"Like hell they do," Hawk spat, her own blade appearing in her hand. It looked tiny, inadequate in this place of monstrous power, but she wielded it like an extension of her own fierce spirit.

"Stone Fist," the acolyte continued, pointedly ignoring Hawk. "This is Temple business. Return to Scalvaris. These outsiders broke our laws."

My wings flared wide, a silent, deadly promise.

"They are under my protection." The words were edged with ice.

The acolyte's face hardened. "The Council wavers. The Temple stands firm. Stand aside or face the consequences—"

Her words were devoured by a piercing screech that tore through the air—the unmistakable hunting cry of Ignarath warriors committing to attack. They plummeted from the ridge, six hurtling shapes of death, wings angled for a killing dive.

No more words. No more posturing.

There was only the howl of the wind and the promise of bloodshed.

"Protect them!" I roared at Hawk, shoving her towards the fallen humans. My eyes locked with Zarvash's. "With me!"

We'd flown ahead of our warriors to scout. I had to hope they would catch up soon. There was no time to wait.

I launched upwards, a coiled spring of muscle and fury unleashed. The first Ignarath met me in a devastating collision, momentum carrying us down in a spiral of claws and snapping teeth. His talons raked my shoulder, drawing hot blood. I roared, a primal sound of challenge echoing off the spires, twisting violently, my tail smashing into his side, sending him tumbling away, disoriented.

Below, the plateau erupted. The yellow-robed cowards scattered like startled insects, scrambling back towards the tunnels that would lead to the city, abandoning the humans they'd captured. Disgust curled my lip.

Hawk and Vega moved with practiced economy, reaching the prone figures, blades flashing as they formed a defensive line, back-to-back. Zarvash landed like a thunderclap beside them and the Ignarath ground assault, his sword a blur of deadly bronze light.

Every instinct screamed at me to drop, to stand beside my mate, to shield her body with my own. But the sky held three more circling predators, waiting to pick us off. Two others engaged Zarvash, their heavier frames giving them brute force advantages.

"Khorlar!" Hawk's voice, sharp with alarm, cut through the din. "More! East!"

A glance confirmed it. Another wave, at least four Ignarath warriors, pounding across the broken ground towards the melee. It was coordinated. Deliberate.

A slaughter planned. And we had walked right into it.

I dove, intercepting a circling warrior, slamming into him with bone-jarring force. We tumbled earthward, a chaotic knot of wings and fury. I twisted at the last second, using his bulk to cushion my impact. The crack of his spine against the stone was grimly satisfying. He didn't move.

There was no time. The remaining two airborne attackers were on me, their movements synchronized, pressing me back. Claws scored my back, ripping through scale. Agony flared as fangs sank deep into the membrane of my left wing.

Rage surged, white-hot and absolute. I roared, spinning, my tail whipping around like a living weapon. It connected with sickening force against one warrior's throat. He collapsed, choking, claws scrabbling at his crushed windpipe. The other lunged, driving me toward the shimmering edge of a sulfur pool, his face a mask of triumphant hatred.

"The humans die!" he snarled, spittle flying. "And the traitors who shield them!"

"Try," I growled back, feinting, then driving forward, my claws finding the vulnerable hollow beneath his jaw. Hot blood sprayed across my chest. His eyes widened, surprised, then glazed over as the light faded.

I spun, desperate, scanning the chaos. Zarvash

fought like a whirlwind of bronze death, his blade weaving intricate patterns, leaving bleeding Ignarath in his wake. Vega stood guard over the fallen, her small knife darting with surprising lethality.

And Hawk—

There. Locked in combat with an Ignarath easily twice her mass. She moved like quicksilver, impossibly fast, her human agility a startling counterpoint to his brute strength. Her blade flashed, biting deep into his exposed side. Dark blood splattered her arm.

A surge of fierce, possessive pride roared through me. My vrakasha. My warrior mate.

Then I saw it. The second attacker. He was closing on her blind side.

She sensed him, turning, but a fraction too late. His massive, rock-hard fist slammed into her ribs. The sound—a sickening crunch—echoed across the battlefield, louder than the cries and the clash of steel. It stopped my heart.

She staggered, her face twisting in a mask of agony, but somehow, impossibly, she stayed on her feet. Pivoting on pure instinct, she drove her blade upward, burying it hilt-deep in the attacker's throat with a final, desperate surge of strength. Blood erupted, drenching her. The Ignarath gurgled, collapsing at her feet.

But she wavered, one arm clamped tight around her side. Even from yards away, I saw the unnatural bulge beneath the harness, the way her body listed.

Something inside me fractured. Shattered into a million razor-sharp pieces.

Thought ceased. Strategy vanished. There was only her.

I launched myself across the battlefield, a meteor of black scales and unrestrained fury. Two more Ignarath moved to block me. They might as well have tried to stop an avalanche. I tore through them. One shrieked as I sheared his wing off at the shoulder in a spray of gore. The other met a stone outcrop with enough force to liquefy his spine. I felt the bones give way under my grip.

I reached her just as her knees buckled. My arms swept around her, rage warring with a desperate tenderness I didn't know I possessed. I lowered her gently, carefully, beside the still forms of her friends.

"Fine," she gasped, her face bleached white, lips bloodless save for a thin trickle leaking from one corner. "Just ... winded ..."

Liar. It tore at me. Through the dark fabric of her undershirt, a bruise was already blooming, deep purple even against her dark skin. Her breathing hitched, shallow and painful. Internal damage. Severe.

Cold terror, absolute and paralyzing, seized me, threatening to freeze me solid. Not a scratch. Not a bruise. This ... this could kill her.

"Hold on." The growl rumbled deep inside me, raw with fear. I scooped her up, cradling her against me, agonizingly aware of her broken ribs, her fragile human frame. "Just hold on, *vrakasha*. Stay with me."

Zarvash materialized beside me, smeared with blood, his breathing harsh. "Go!" he commanded, his sharp eyes taking in Hawk's pallor, the blood at her mouth. "Healing caverns. Now. We'll handle this."

No argument. No hesitation. My wings beat the air with frantic power, thrusting us skyward. I held her tight, the harness that had earlier felt like betrayal now the only thing keeping her secure against my desperate flight. Each shallow, shuddering breath she took rippled against my chest, a counterpoint to the frantic pounding of my own heart.

She was dying. My mate. Dying in my arms.

Panic clawed at me, raw and blinding, making my flight path unsteady. Faster. I needed to fly faster. My wings strained, muscles screaming, driving us through the darkening sky towards the distant glow of Scalvaris. Towards the healers. Towards hope.

"Stay with me," I commanded again, the words rough, torn from my throat. "That is an order, *vrakasha*. Do you hear me? Stay. With. Me."

Her eyelids fluttered. Her gaze was unfocused, clouded with pain, but she found mine. "Not ... taking orders ...," she rasped, a faint echo of her infuriating defiance flickering through the agony, "from you ..."

A strangled sound ripped from me, caught somewhere between a laugh and a sob. "Stubborn ... always stubborn ..."

"Not ... the end ...," she whispered, her fingers weakly clutching the harness strap across my chest. "Not ... letting you ... win ... that easily ..."

Scalvaris loomed. I didn't slow, didn't signal. I arrowed straight towards the opening that led deep into the mountain, towards the life-giving heat of the healing caverns.

She would not die. I refused it. The bond pulsed, a desperate anchor in the storm of my fear. I would tear down the mountain stone by stone before I let her fade. She would not die.

DARKNESS PRESSED DOWN. I fought my way up through it, clawing against a pressure inside me that made it feel like I was drowning even though I was miles from water. Sound bled in first—low murmurs, alien and guttural. The soft, grating clink of metal on stone. Then sensation—a raw, grinding throb between my ribs, pulsing like a second, jagged heartbeat. Bandages scraped rough against skin. And heat. A thick, ambient heat that clung to everything.

My eyelids were fused shut. I forced them open, blinking against the glare of heat crystals dotting the cavern ceiling like embers. Panic detonated—a pure adrenaline dump before memory caught up. The ambush. Stone shattering. Ignarath claws ripping air. Pain exploding through my chest like a shaped charge. Khorlar—

I tried to surge upright, a feral instinct to move, but hands clamped down, firm and unyielding. My vision swam, focusing slowly on Selene's face—sharp angles, brown skin, eyes that missed nothing.

"Easy," she murmured, her voice low. It was steady and clinical. Her fingers probed the bandages wrapping my torso. "Move like that, and you tear the sutures." It was blunt and practical.

Reality slammed back. I remembered the sickening crunch of my own bones. I tasted the copper tang of blood flooding my mouth. I heard the roar that had ripped from Khorlar's throat as I went down —a sound primal enough to shake the stone. My heart hammered against the cage of my ribs, each beat agony.

"Khorlar," I rasped, the word torn from a raw throat. "Where—? Is he—?" The question died. I couldn't ask it.

"He's fine," Selene said. A minuscule tilt of her head indicated the space beside me. "There."

I turned my head. Muscles screamed, protesting the simple movement. Pain lanced through me, sharp and immediate. But the sight stopped my breath cold.

He sprawled on a wide stone slab nearby, his immense form terrifyingly still. His power was leashed by exhaustion. One wing, its leathery membrane marred by neat, precise stitches—Selene's work—draped off the edge, inert. His chest rose and fell, slow, deep. Gray scales drank the molten light.

He was alive. Not broken.

Relief hit like a physical blow. Weakness flooded me, dizzying and unwelcome. My gaze traced the lines of his face, unguarded in sleep, the harsh angles softened. A rare, dangerous vulnerability.

"What—" I cleared my throat, forcing the words past the knot tightening there. "What happened?"

Selene's fingers continued their assessment, efficient, detached. "You took a killing strike. Your lung collapsed. There was severe internal bleeding." Her eyes, dark and direct, met mine. No softening. "Three ribs fractured." She paused, letting the starkness land. "He carried you to the healing caverns. Just in time."

Just in time. Those were words like ice picks. A breath away from too late. The abyss yawned.

"The others?" I demanded, gritting my teeth against the relentless throb.

"Stable. Kira is recovering from sedation. Minor injuries elsewhere." Her expression tightened almost imperceptibly. "Reika and Rachel are already back in their quarters, they were just knocked out."

My eyes kept dragging back to Khorlar. There was an invisible tether to him. "Is he hurt?" I couldn't filter the edge from my voice. Couldn't pretend indifference.

"It's exhaustion. Lacerations and wing tears." Selene's mouth twitched, a fleeting acknowledgment of something complex passing between warrior and healer. "He refused treatment until I confirmed your life-signs stabilized. Refused to leave this slab until he physically collapsed. I threatened to sedate him. It took Mysha coming in here and staring him down to get him to back off."

Something hot and volatile coiled low in my gut, unrelated to the pain. The thought of him, standing guard, bleeding, refusing aid while I hovered near death ... The image pulsed through me, a dangerous resonance. Control slipping.

"How long?" I needed the measure of the gap. Needed to know the time stolen.

"Long enough," Selene replied. "I'm still learning Drakarn healing, but they have some out of this world herbs. It accelerated your healing. It looks like you've been recovering for weeks, not days. But you are far from recovered."

My fingers brushed the thick layers wrapped

around my torso. It felt like a cage of gauze. "I need to—"

"You need to rest," she cut me off, sharp as flint. Then her gaze softened fractionally, following mine to Khorlar. "Although ... proximity has its own restorative properties, it seems."

Heat crawled up my neck. Proximity. It was a clinical word for something raw and unnamed. "He needs to know," I muttered, the admission escaping before I could lock it down.

Selene nodded. "Can you stand? The pain will be severe."

Every movement was fire. Agony licked along my ribs, grinding bone on bone with each hitched breath. But Selene's grip was steel beneath my elbow, an impersonal support. The need to reach him was a physical force, overriding pain, overriding reason. It was a gravity I couldn't fight. When we reached the edge of his slab, I hesitated, suddenly adrift in the space between wounded animal and ... something else.

"I have other patients." Selene released my arm, her voice quiet but firm. "Do not compromise my work, Hawk."

She slipped away into the shadows, leaving me swaying, the air thick with Khorlar's heat and scent.

Up close, the scale of him was staggering. Hard muscle lay beneath gray plates, the sharp line of his jaw relaxed in sleep, one arm flung outward, palm up, claws loose. Reaching.

For me.

The thought struck like lightning. This warrior. This alien predator. He'd smashed through every defense, breached every wall I'd ever built. He had carved out territory inside me where none should exist. Watching the slow rise and fall of his chest, feeling that inexorable pull, I knew it with chilling certainty. There was no going back.

Every instinct honed for survival, for self-reliance, screamed betrayal. Silenced by something older. Deeper. More savage.

Mine. His claim, echoed back from my own core.

Deliberately, gritting my teeth against the fire, I lowered myself onto the edge of the warm stone. No hesitation now. I eased down beside him, fitting myself into the curve of his massive body, sliding under the shelter of that outstretched arm.

Contact sent a shockwave through me. It wasn't pain, but ignition. His body radiated heat like a furnace core, seeping into my chilled marrow, driving out a coldness I hadn't known I carried. I rested my head against the solid wall of his chest.

The steady rhythm of his heart pulsed against my ear —stronger, deeper than human. Thrumming.

It felt like surrender. Like stepping into the heart of the sun. Terrifyingly like home.

My eyelids turned to lead. Exhaustion, heavy and absolute, dragged me under. Here. Beside him. Safe wasn't the word. Claimed felt closer. Marked.

I surfaced later to movement. A sharp inhale beneath my ear. Tension snapped through the arm under my head, muscle turning to stone. Molten gold eyes flared open, shock locking his features as he stared down at me.

"*Vrakasha*," he breathed, the Drakarn word vibrating against my cheek. It was rough and possessive. His free hand hovered near my face, claws extended but unsteady. Trembling? "You live."

A faint smile pulled at my lips, cracking the mask of pain. "Apparently. You too."

His nostrils flared, drawing in my scent, assessing me in that wild, unnerving way. His arm tightened— a brief, crushing pressure—then instantly eased as memory of my injuries surfaced. He was careful now. Lethally careful.

"I thought ..." His voice was raw, stripped bare. Unfiltered. "When you were struck ... I felt the bones give beneath my hands." A shudder wracked his frame, immense power momentarily losing purchase. "I did not understand fear. Not until then."

"Takes more than a little fight to get rid of me," I murmured. I aimed for defiance. Landed somewhere raw. Vulnerable. Hated it.

His hand settled in my hair, claws impossibly gentle against my scalp, mapping the short strands. Confirming reality. "I cannot lose you." Simple. Stark. Absolute. "It would break me."

The confession wasn't emotional weakness. It was structural truth. Gouged in bedrock. This creature of fire and violence, tethering his existence to mine. My absence wasn't loss. It was annihilation.

Terror should have seized me. Sent me scrambling for distance, for the hard-won isolation that kept soldiers alive.

Instead, my own hand rose, ignoring the screaming protest of stitches. I traced the sharp ridge of his jaw. Solid reality under my fingertips. "I'm not going anywhere," I promised. A vow torn from me, echoing his intensity. "Not now. Not ever."

His eyes flared, pupils swallowing the gold. Pure predator. He leaned down, pressing his forehead to mine. It was more intimate than any kiss. His breath washed over my face—stone dust, ozone, Khorlar.

"When you are healed," he rumbled, the sound

vibrating deep in his chest, a physical force. "I will claim you. Properly. Before all. There will be no doubt." A statement of intent. Unshakeable. "You are mine."

The promise, raw, absolute, sent a tremor through me that had nothing to do with injury. My fingers tightened on his jaw. Acceptance. Challenge. Agreement.

"I'm counting on it," I whispered back, the words tasting like recklessness.

His answering growl rumbled through my bones. Pure, male satisfaction. His arms shifted, cradling me with infinite care against the solid heat of his chest. His wing settled over us, a living shield of black membrane and scaled muscle, cocooning us in shadow and warmth.

"Sleep," he commanded, the word rough-edged, possessive. Almost gentle. "Heal. I'll watch."

Wrapped in his heat, anchored by the steady beat of his heart, I let myself sink. Into the certainty of his presence. Into the terrifying, exhilarating knowledge that I'd found something immense, unbreakable, dangerous. Here. In this violent world.

In him.

"By the First Flame's boiling blood, this is a healing sanctuary, not a ... a nesting ground!"

The voice, sharp as obsidian shards, sliced through the warm dark. Yanked me back to awareness. Pain flared, hot and immediate, across my ribs. A female Drakarn stood at the foot of the slab, scales shimmering with indignation, wings flared tight with disapproval. Mysha. The head healer. Crystal adornments woven into her head-frills chimed with her rigid stance.

"Six hours! I attend the lower caverns for six hours, and I return to find my most critical patients ... entwined!" My translator offered "entwined." Her tone suggested "fucking like rabbits."

A choked sound escaped me—half laugh, half gasp of pain. Khorlar's arm tightened instinctively, a low growl vibrating against my back, possessive and immediate.

"She required comfort," he rumbled, deep, unwavering. Stating fact. Like gravity.

"Comfort?" Mysha sputtered, frills flaring wider, radiating annoyance like heat waves. "Survival protocols dictate minimal contact, not ... cuddling!"

I pushed myself up slightly, wincing as stitches pulled. "To be fair, I'm pretty sure my blood's exactly where it's supposed to be now." Sarcasm as armor.

Mysha's glare could have cracked granite. "Humor. From a human. While recovering from near-fatal trauma. Excellent." She stalked closer, the healer overriding the outraged elder. Her gaze swept over my bandages, clinical, assessing. "Do you have any breathing difficulty? Sharp pain on inhalation? Vertigo?"

"Just ... sore," I admitted, hating the concession. Letting her check the bindings with claws that, despite their sharpness, moved with practiced gentleness. "Like something large and pissed off used my ribs for target practice."

"Hmph," she sniffed, though her claws were deft, "but the impact trauma was ... significant." She straightened, frills settling fractionally. "Your human physiology metabolizes the restorative minerals with unexpected efficiency." A grudging admission.

"I'm cleared for duty, then?" I shot back, hope a stubborn weed despite the grinding ache.

Khorlar's growl dropped lower, gaining a menacing edge. "No." Absolute. Final.

"That is my determination, Stone Fist," Mysha snapped back, though a flicker of something— approval? respect for his claim?—crossed her sharp features. She looked back at me. "Light duty. Minimal exertion. No combat maneuvers. No flight stressors. And no activities which might ... place undue strain ... on the regenerating tissues." Her gaze flicked between us, pointed and unambiguous.

Heat flooded my face. Damn her clinical precision. "Understood."

"See that you both do." Mysha gathered her implements, crystals tinkling like fractured ice. "Now, remove yourselves from my primary healing chamber. I have actual invalids requiring attention, not ... bonded pairs treating sacred restorative spaces like personal territory."

"Bonded?" The word hit like a physical weight, settling deep in my chest. Irrevocable.

Mysha rolled her eyes, a startlingly human gesture on that alien face. "Please. The bond-scent radiating from you both is thick enough to taste. It disrupts the chamber's healing harmonics." She flicked her tail dismissively, a gesture of finality. "Out. Now. Before I decide a vivisection would yield more useful data than your convalescence."

She turned sharply, muttering about "disrespectful off-worlders," "primal preoccupations," and "improper nesting instincts," stalking towards another alcove, radiating disapproval.

I looked up at Khorlar. Found a rare spark of something like amusement softening the hard lines of his face. Dangerous territory, that softness. "Bond-scent?" I asked, raising an eyebrow despite the pull of stitches. Testing the word.

His amusement vanished. Replaced by that molten intensity that stole the air from my lungs. His gaze locked on mine. Burning. "Yes," he rumbled, the word heavy. Certain. "Undeniable. Unmistakable." His hand came up, claws tracing the line of my jaw, possessive heat sinking into my skin. Branding. "Mine."

Without thought, without resistance, accepting the inevitable gravity, I leaned into his touch. "Yours," I whispered. The word felt like stepping off a cliff into fire. His eyes promised I wouldn't burn alone.

"Let's get out of here," I added, voice steadier than the ground felt beneath me, "before she comes back with something sharp and experimental."

"THESE ARE MY PERSONAL CHAMBERS," Khorlar growled, the sound vibrating low in his chest. His claws flexed on the doorframe, exhibiting a hesitation so unlike him it snagged my attention. "Our chambers. Now."

The claim wasn't soft. It landed like a brand, heat flaring low in my belly instead of the expected prickle of resentment. Stepping inside felt like crossing a boundary I couldn't see. The air clung, heavy with his scent—not just the familiar ozone and dust of the tunnels, but something richer, the tang of forge-heat deep in the stone, charred cedar after rain, and an undercurrent of raw musk that coated the back of my throat. Mine. The word echoed in the scent, in the weight of the air.

Weapon racks lined one wall, and the steel

wasn't just gleaming—it looked hungry, used. The wooden grips were dark with oil and countless grips of his hand. They were not decorative. They were ready. Geological maps etched into stone panels weren't just art; they pulsed with faint geothermal light, the lines sharp enough to cut. Every surface seemed charged with his presence.

His eyes—molten gold, predatory—tracked my every step across the floor. It wasn't cold stone; warmth radiated up, a low thrum of power from the planet's core, more potent here. More intimate. That gaze didn't feel like targeting anymore. It felt like ... ownership. Devouring.

"Is this acceptable?" he asked, the gravel in his voice rougher, laced with something that scraped like uncertainty. This, from the male who'd torn through soldiers like they were paper? The vulnerability was a shock, sharp and disorienting.

"It's you," I managed, turning. The admission felt ripped from me, raw and too loud in the sudden quiet. "I feel you. Everywhere."

His nostrils flared, sampling the air between us, tasting my scent, my reaction. His jaw tightened, satisfied. He stalked closer, heat rolling off him in waves, the air crackling. In three strides, he filled my space, dwarfing me.

"There is no one else," he admitted, his words clipped, rough. "This was ... mine. Only mine. Until you."

The weight of it pressed down. It was not just sharing space. This was sanctuary breached, walls lowered. His last defense. Offered.

We didn't talk about the med-bay, the blood, the sickening crack of my bones beneath his desperate hands trying to hold me together. We didn't need to. Death's cold shadow lingered, making the heat between us flare brighter, more desperate. Everything flimsy between us had burned away in that sterile white room, leaving only this raw, jagged truth.

He moved again, closing the last inch. His hand came up, claws clicking softly as they hesitated near my face. Then, impossibly gentle for such lethal weapons, the pads of his scaled fingers brushed stray hair from my cheek. Electricity didn't just skitter; it jolted through me, bypassing the dull throb in my ribs to pool, hot and heavy, low in my gut.

My breath hitched.

His eyes locked on mine. Gold burned into brown. He was not the Stone Fist. Not the Council member. Just Khorlar. Raw. Gutted. His heart beat a frantic rhythm I could almost *feel* in the air. Offered up like a sacrifice.

Words were useless. Ash in the mouth. My hand lifted, clumsy, touching his jaw. The scales weren't smooth; they were textured, warm ridges over unyielding bone. Real. Solid. Here.

Something shattered between us—not tension, but the last brittle restraint. We collided, drawn by a force that was beyond choice.

His mouth met mine, not soft, but possessive. A desperate claiming that tasted of relief and the lingering metallic tang of fear. His fear. For me. This wasn't reverence; it was raw need, a staking of claim on what was almost lost. My hands fisted in the coarse fabric of his tunic, pulling him closer, needing the solid weight of him.

"*Vrakasha,*" he groaned against my lips. His hands clamped onto my waist, fingers digging slightly, careful of the bandages but demanding contact. He was learning me again, not with wonder, but with the frantic desperation of confirming I was whole. Real.

I answered with touch, not words. My palms scraped over the hard planes of his chest, scale ridges catching against my skin. The thump of his heart slammed against my hand, a frantic drumbeat mirroring my own pulse.

He deepened the kiss, his tongue sweeping into my mouth—hot, insistent, tasting me, marking me. He was exploring not with tenderness, but with a starved urgency.

He broke the kiss only to lift me. There was no warning, just solid muscle bunching as he scooped me against his chest. My ribs screamed a reminder, but the pain was distant, drowned by the crushing safety of his hold. His wings flared, shadowing us, creating a sudden, intimate darkness as he strode toward the massive sleeping platform dominating the far side of the room.

This wasn't the sparse cot of the siege room. Thick silks—black, midnight blue, deep gray— covered a carved stone base. A predator's nest. He laid me down, not like crystal, but like something vital he couldn't bear to drop. His claws scraped lightly against my hip as he straightened.

"The bindings—" he started, his voice tight, gaze fixed on the white bandages stark against my skin.

I cut him off, fingers already fumbling with the clasp of my tunic. "Off," I said. It was not a request. It was a demand. "Slow. I need to feel."

His eyes flared hotter, pupils dilating until only a

thin rim of gold remained. He didn't rush. He backed off, giving me space, but his gaze ... his gaze stripped me bare faster than my own fingers could.

My shirt came off with a wince, the movement pulling at healing tissue. His breath sawed out, a harsh sound. It was not desire, not yet. It was the sight of the bandages—the proof of my fragility, of how close he'd come to failure. His claws flexed, gouging shallow lines into his own thigh.

"Here," I whispered, the word thin. "I'm here."

He gave a single, jerky nod. Then his hands went to his own armor. Buckles hissed, straps fell away, and heavy leather dropped onto the stone floor. It was not a ritual. It was a shedding of restraint. Piece by painful piece until he stood there, lit by the pulsing light of the heat crystals. Naked. Power coiled tight under black and gray scales that gleamed like wet volcanic rock. They thinned over the hard ridges of his abdomen, hinting at darker skin beneath. His cock, already thick and half-hard, jutted from its scaled base, flushed a brutal crimson, twitching. A drop of clear fluid beaded at the angry-looking slit at the tip.

I expected him to lunge. To pin me down and reclaim me with bruising force. Instead, he lowered himself onto the furs beside me, facing me. Close enough that his heat scorched my skin. One hand, claws carefully averted, landed heavy on my hip. His tail snaked around my ankle, a possessive weight. Grounding. Claiming.

"There are no words," he grated out, his voice raw. "My tongue ... has no words for this." He gestured between us, the air thick with unspoken need.

My throat closed. I swallowed, hard. "Then show me." The whisper was ragged.

He leaned in, mouth brushing my forehead, my temple, the corner of my lips. Each touch wasn't reverent—it was branding. Testing. His hand slid up my side, heat searing through the thin bandage wrap, stopping just below my breast. Then his palm covered me, thumb scraping, rasping over the peak through the fabric until it beaded tight, aching.

I gasped, arching, pressing into the abrasive touch. My own hands moved, starved for contact. Scraping over scale ridges, finding the surprising heat where wing met back, the vulnerable thinness of scale near his flanks. Every touch ripped a reaction from him—a hiss of breath, muscles bunching, a low growl rumbling against my exploring hand.

My fingers snagged on a raised line of scar tissue

across his bicep—pale against the dark scales. "What about this?" I murmured, tracing the puckered ridge.

His eyes went distant for a second, then focused, hard. "That was first blood," he clipped out. "I was young. Stupid. Ignarath filth nearly took the arm."

My thumb pressed down, acknowledging the violence, the survival. "And this one?" Near his collarbone, another mark, smoother.

A rough sound, almost a chuckle, vibrated through his chest. "That was Thrakas. My brother." His expression shuttered. "Training. Always too fast."

The glimpse behind the armor, into the male forged by violence and loss ... it wasn't a gift. It was a weapon surrendered. I leaned in, pressed my lips to the collarbone scar, tasting salt and old pain.

His breath hitched, sharp. His hand tangled in my hair, fingers tight, anchoring me as I tasted another scar on his shoulder, fresh, still pink beneath the scales—from the fight. From saving me. My tongue traced the ragged edge. An apology. A promise.

"No," he growled, catching my wrist, his grip bruisingly tight before easing almost instantly. "These scars? I bear them proudly." His gaze burned. "They are the price. For what's mine."

The word detonated low in my belly. I surged up, crashing my mouth against his, pouring everything—fear, gratitude, raw, aching need—into the kiss. His answering growl was pure possession, his arms crushing me against him, ignoring the faint protest of my ribs. Distance was intolerable.

His hands mapped me, not gently, but with greedy haste. His fingers dug into the curve of my waist, thumb brushing the edge of the bandages. He found the small scar on my shoulder, a relic of a stupid training accident. He broke the kiss, examining it like an enemy's mark.

"Who did this?" he demanded, tracing it, his claw tip scoring the skin beside it.

I shook my head, a shaky laugh escaping. "Gravity. A failed harness."

His growl was guttural, furious at the inanimate object that dared injure me. His mouth replaced his claw, sucking lightly at the old scar, a possessive claiming that sent shivers down my spine.

We mapped each other like that—scar tissue and healed wounds laid bare. Stories told in touch and ragged breaths. His wings curved, enclosing us further, a stifling cocoon of heat and shadow. Just us. Skin, scale, sweat, and the frantic hammer of his heart.

His hand slid lower, between my thighs. He found me slick, hot, ready. His growl wasn't approval. It was triumph. His touch wasn't gentle teasing. It was direct, demanding. His fearsome claws sheathed, but the pressure of his fingers was insistent, circling, pressing, gathering the wet heat before zeroing in on my clit. One rough slide of his thumb.

I cried out, hips bucking hard off the furs. "Khor-lar!" His name was torn from me, half plea, half curse.

"I've got you, *vrakasha*," he rasped, his voice thick, strained. "Always."

He didn't explore. He took. While his finger could tease, the claw made it too dangerous to go inside. But he had his tail. Opening me. Stretching me. Making me desperate for more. A broken sound clawed its way up my throat. I writhed against him, desperate, impatient.

My own hand closed around his cock. It was thick. Hotter than seemed possible. Veins like cords beneath skin that felt rougher, more textured than human. The blunt tip pulsed against my palm, the lip-like ridge there twitching, weeping more slick fluid that smelled of ozone and musk. Need coiled tight, sharp, demanding in my core.

I couldn't take the slow torment. I tugged him, hard. "Now," I choked out against his jaw. "Need you. Now."

He shifted, levering himself between my thighs. Careful of my ribs, but the movement was still brutally efficient. His wings tented over us, trapping the heat, the scent, the tension. Amber light filtered through the membranes, throwing his harsh features into stark relief. He positioned the thick, blunt head of his cock at my entrance.

"Mine," he snarled, the word ripped from his throat as he surged forward. He was not easing in. He was invading. Stretching me wide, a burning fullness that bordered on pain. "My mate. My heart."

The words, raw, desperate, shattered something inside me. Tears sprang, hot and sudden, blurring the sight of his face above mine. He filled me completely, a sweet, agonizing ache.

He started to move. Deep, powerful thrusts that stole my breath. There was no finesse. Pure claiming. That ridge at the tip of his cock dragged against my clit with every stroke, a brutal, exquisite friction that sent sparks behind my eyes. His tail tightened around my ankle, pulsing with each jarring impact.

"You are perfect," he grated out, his voice dropping lower, vibrating through the pelts, through me. "Take me ... like you were made for this. For me."

It wasn't possession. It was ... inevitability. Fate. I clawed at his shoulders, rising to meet him, take him deeper. My nails scraped against scale, seeking purchase.

He lowered his head, teeth grazing the junction of my neck and shoulder. It was not a kiss. It was a mark. A promise. "When you heal," he vowed, his breath scorching my skin, "I will mark you. Properly. So all know."

A bolt of pure heat shot through me, my inner muscles clenching around him convulsively. He threw his head back, a guttural groan tearing from his chest.

"Yes," I gasped, not knowing what I agreed to, only that I wanted it. Him. This. Everything. "Yours."

His rhythm shattered. His control snapped. The next thrust slammed into me, driving the air from my lungs, hitting something deep that splintered my vision. "Again," he demanded, his voice cracking.

"Yours!" I sobbed, the word freeing something wild inside me. "And you—mine!"

His roar was triumph, pure and feral. He shifted, one hand shoving under my hips, tilting me, changing the angle. Driving deeper. Harder. Stars exploded behind my eyes. White-hot. Searing.

The climax slammed into me, not a wave, but a brutal rip tide, dragging me under. Thought ceased. Breath ceased. There was only the searing friction, the agonizing pleasure, the feeling of being filled, claimed, owned. His name tore from my throat, unrecognizable.

He followed me down, his own control shattering. Triggered by my convulsing muscles, his release ripped through him. His head arched back, wings flaring violently as he roared, the sound bouncing off the stone, shaking the very air. His seed flooded me, thick, scalding hot, branding me from the inside out as his hips bucked one last time.

He didn't collapse. He shuddered, catching his weight on trembling arms before carefully rolling us to our sides, pulling me tight against his chest. His wings folded around us, a heavy, living blanket trapping the sweat, the scent, the aftermath.

"I thought …," he choked out, the words rough against my hair. "I thought I lost you. Saw you hurt. Felt … felt the break." A violent shudder wracked his frame. "Nothing … nothing ever …"

I pressed my palm flat against the frantic beat of

his heart. "I'm hard to kill," I whispered, trying for levity, failing.

His arm became a vise. "Anchor," he rasped, ignoring me. "My fire. Without ..." He couldn't finish.

The jagged honesty tore through my remaining defenses. Here, wrapped in his heat, shielded by his body, I let the vulnerability surface. Let it crack me open.

"I never expected this," I admitted, the words small, fragile. "You. Drakarn. Home." I swallowed the lump in my throat. "It should be wrong. Alien." My fingers trembled as they traced the hard line of his jaw. "It feels ... terrifyingly right. Like finding something I didn't know I was looking for."

He caught my hand, pressing his mouth to my palm, the touch searing. "Mate," he rumbled, the sound deep, resonant. "The heart knows. It is not a choice. It is recognition." His golden eyes, no longer alien, just intensely *him*, bored into mine. "You are mine. As I am yours. Not chance. Fate."

The certainty didn't frighten me now. It settled deep, a heavy, warm anchor in the chaos. Peace. Acceptance. This impossible place. This impossible male. Home.

I pushed myself up slightly, pressing my mouth

to his. It was not passion now. It was a seal. A silent vow exchanged in taste and touch.

Sleep pulled at me, heavy and sudden. As darkness claimed the edges, I felt his lips brush my forehead, rough scales scraping gently. "Rest, *vrakasha*," he murmured, the sound a low rumble against my skull. "Heal. I am here."

The promise wrapped around me tighter than his wings, a bulwark against the lingering chill of the void. And, finally, I surrendered.

THE DARKNESS WAS ABSOLUTE.

It was an oppressive weight crushing vision, heavier than any sleep. This void was an insult, a cage built of stolen light. Then, there was agony. It seared through my skull like shattered obsidian, radiating from where scales were scraped raw against something cold.

I fought the blackness, tried to command limbs that refused to answer. I was bound. The tight, coarse material bit deep, grinding against hide, against bone. Humiliation burned hotter than the pain. My wings were in violation. They were wrenched back, twisted grotesquely, joints screaming a silent protest. Panic, cold and sharp, clawed at my throat.

To be grounded ... trapped. A warrior stripped of his sky is less than nothing.

The metallic tang of my own blood coated my tongue. Salt and iron. Fury coiled tight in my gut. I carefully worked my jaw, ignoring the fresh pulse of agony through my skull. I was unbroken. It was a small mercy in this degradation.

"... waste of resources ..." The voice grated, harsh and thick with the unmistakable, sloppy cadence of the Ignarath. It was like stones scraping stone. Contemptible.

"Orders are orders." The second voice was smoother yet carried the same underlying arrogance. "They pay well for live ones."

Live ones. Tactical awareness cut through the pain. I forced my breathing shallow, even. Stillness was a shield; information, a blade waiting to be drawn. I let them think me broken.

"The female's useless," the first grunted, closer now. The scrape of his talons on unseen stone set my teeth on edge. "Human. She won't survive."

Human? The word struck like a physical blow. Female. Images fractured behind the darkness—the scouting mission, the sudden chaos, Ignarath filth pouring from the rocks. Was it Kira? No ... Terra? Darrokar's mate? Impossible. He would have leveled this mountain range. Who else? Khorlar would have died fighting. Who?

A guttural snort followed. "It's double price for humans now."

Then, something else cut through the stench of blood and the cold dampness of the stone. A scent bloomed in the stale air, impossibly sweet, complex. It was like fire-nectar blooms, yes, but laced with something ... alien. Utterly foreign, yet it resonated deep within my bones, a vibration beneath the pain. My nostrils flared, drawing it in against my will. It invaded my senses like fine smoke, bypassing thought, settling somewhere primal. My fangs ached —a sharp, unfamiliar pang. The very air seemed to thicken, growing textured against my tongue.

"Check the bronze one's restraints," the calmer voice commanded, closer now. "He's dangerous."

Heavy talons scraped stone, approaching. Every instinct screamed to tear free, to rend and shatter, but I forced stillness. Weakness is a cloak.

"Still out," the first grunted. "I hit him hard enough." A sharp prod dug into my shoulder, finding a raw wound I hadn't fully registered. Pain flared, white-hot. I clamped my jaw, biting back the reflexive growl, tasting blood anew.

Then the scent intensified. It was overwhelming.

Closer. Something warm, impossibly soft, pressed against my side. Heat radiated through thin fabric, against my scales. Not stone. Not metal. Life. Small, rhythmic breaths, too fast for my kind. A human. Her. The realization struck like lightning, rearranging the landscape of my pain.

The scent poured from her, wrapping around my senses, drowning the stench of Ignarath and damp rock. It fogged my thoughts, pulling focus with a magnetic force, an undertow dragging me toward something ancient and absolute.

"He's waking up," a voice snarled from my other side. A vicious kick landed squarely on my ribs, stealing my breath. "Dose him again."

"Waste of venom. Exchange by nightfall."

Movement beside me indicated she stirred, the woman—the source of the scent. A soft sound, feminine, fragile, bypassed reason, striking a deep, resonant chord within my chest. It was possessive. Primal. My muscles bunched, straining futilely against the unyielding bindings.

"Separate them," the calmer one ordered sharply. "He's reacting. I've seen this filth before."

"Disgusting," spat the first. "Scalvaris heathens. Mating with off-worlders." Another kick slammed into my wounded side, fueled by contempt.

She made another sound. It was pained. A soft whimper that ignited a bonfire of fury within me. A growl tore from my throat, low and vicious, shattering my facade of unconsciousness. I was exposed.

"See? Told you." Rough hands fumbled near my head, grabbing at the binding over my eyes, then pausing. "Leave him blind. It's less trouble."

"Move her."

"No ...," her voice came. Barely a whisper, yet it resonated through my bones like a struck shield. A challenge. A claim?

Hands seized her, dragging the warmth, the scent, away. Panic, raw and illogical, clawed through me. The sudden emptiness beside me was an agony sharper than any physical wound. The scent faded, pulling my focus, my strength, with it.

"Stop ..." The word was a broken rasp, torn from my throat. Darkness surged at the edges of the void, thicker now.

Pain pulsed, a relentless hammer against my skull, but beneath it, one imperative burned with the clarity of molten corestone. This pull, this sudden, fierce certainty ... it wasn't confusion. It was recognition. An awakening of something buried deep within the bedrock of my being.

Whoever she was, she belonged under my protection.

I had to find her. Shield her.

She was mine.

The blackness swallowed me whole once more.

―――

Thank you so much for reading *Fated to the Drakarn Commander*!

Your support means the world to me. If you enjoyed the story, it would mean even more if you could take a moment to share your thoughts in a review or leave a rating.

Hearing from readers like you makes all the difference!

NEED A LITTLE MORE OF KHORLAR & HAWK?

Sign up at the link below to **receive a free bonus epilogue!**

Get your freebie!

https://katerudolph.net/index.php/khorlar-bonus/

Drakarn Mates

A HARSH DESERT PLANET. Stranded humans. Draconic aliens. A match made in... well, somewhere.

Claimed by the Drakarn Warrior Lord
Echoes of Fire
Scorched by Fate
Fated to the Drakarn Commander

———

Dragon Brides
Dragon Princes. Fierce Women. Love.

Fated mates, fierce women, and dragon princes are
ready to find their mates.
Also available in audio!
Crux
Ranger
Saber
Cipher
Storm
Drake
Asher
Knox
Flint
Pine

Guarded by the Shifter

Werewolf. Bodyguard. Mate.
The origins of these shifters are shrouded in mystery,
but they're determined to protect their mates from
any harm that comes their way.
Also available in audio!
Hunting Season
On the Prowl
Stalking Magic

Hungry for the Wolf
Wolf Cursed (novella)
Wolf's Temptation

Stealing the Alpha

The thief takes what she wants, but the alpha keeps what's his...

Join shifter thief Mel as she clashes with lion alpha Luke in an explosive trilogy of two opposites who can't keep away from one another.

Also available in audio!

The Alpha Heist
Entangled with the Thief
In the Alpha's Bed

Alien Mates: Planet Exile

Guerran is no place for pretty human women. But these alien heroes will protect their mates!

Also available in audio!

Exile's Hunter

Exile's Adored

————

Zulir Warrior Mates

Kidnapped humans. Alien Warriors. Electric wings.

The Zulir Warrior Mates series brings you human heroines and heroes abducted from Earth who find love – and wings! – with the alien warriors who rescue them.

Also available in audio!

Synnr's Saint

Synnr's Hope

Synnr's Spark

Synnr's Kiss

Synnr's Ride

————

Mated to the Alien

Fated Mate Alien Romance

Detyens are doomed to die young if they don't find their fated mates.

Follow along as these mated pairs fight off aliens, corrupt dictators, prejudiced humans, pirates, and more! The books can be read or listened to in any order, though some characters show up in multiple stories.

Select books available in audio.

Pick a book and jump into the action today!

Ruwen

Tyral

Stoan

Cyborg

Krayter

Kayleb

Shayn

Braxtyn

Doryan

Dekon

Detyen Warriors

Detya was destroyed a hundred years ago.

These doomed warriors are out to find justice… and their mates.

The Detyen Warriors series brings you kick butt heroines, alpha alien heroes, fated mates, and relationships strong enough to span the galaxy!

The entire series is also available in audio!

Soulless

Ruthless

Heartless

Faultless

Endless

Detyen Warrior Outcasts
Fated Mate Alien Romance

These doomed warriors were abandoned by their people and live on the edge. Their mates hold the key to their salvation.

Pick a book and jump into the action today!

Also available in audio!

Dangerous Bond

Intrepid Bond

Wayward Bond

Alien Holiday Romance

Christmas... in space????
These alien holiday romances look beyond Earth's winter holidays and ring in the season across the galaxy!
Select titles available in audio.
Snowed in with the Alien Beast
The Alien's Winter Gift
The Alien Reindeer's Wild Ride
Trapped with her Alien Mate

Alien Outlaws

Outlaws, schemes, and love... it's all there in the Alien Outlaws series...
Andie Munster is sick of life on Ixilta, the planet she got dumped on after being abducted from Earth six years ago. And when the mysterious and dangerous Xandr shows up looking for a way off the planet, she's half-prisoner, half-co-conspirator in a wild rush to escape.

Also available in audio!

Rogue Alien's Escape

Rogue Alien's Woman

Rogue Alien's Secret

Rogue Alien's Legacy

———

Find more by Kate Rudolph at www. katerudolph.net

ABOUT KATE RUDOLPH

KATE RUDOLPH IS a paranormal and sci-fi romance writer who lives in Indiana. She loves writing about kick butt heroines and the steamy heroes who love them. She's been devouring romance novels since she was too young to be reading them and had to hide her books so no one would take them away. She couldn't imagine a better job in this world than writing romances and sharing them with her fellow readers.

If you enjoyed this story, please consider leaving a review.